unplugged

a novella

david schulze

david schulze books | davidschulzebooks.com

David Schulze Books

Modern Myth Trilogy

1. *The Sins of Jack Branson*
2. *Andrezj of Hollywood*
3. *Olive Branch*

Other Fiction

unplugged

ISBN-13
eBook: 978-1-7370378-6-6
Paperback: 979-8-9920574-0-9

It took a while, but we're finally at a place where we can talk, not just as father and son, but as two men finally living the lives we deserve. Let's not lose this. I actually kinda love it.

To John Stehman

"Everyone faces their demons at some point, if not in themselves then in their children."

— an actual comment I found on YouTube

0.

prelude

I never wanted to be a father until today. Bad upbringing, you know. Wanted to end the cycle. And I was just starting out my writing career. Newly married. Not to mention I valued intelligence. I refused to play dumb or let someone win. That required a level of selflessness I knew I was incapable of giving.

But my husband wanted a kid. He's older than I am. Old fashioned. One of those strict monogamy homos. Religious wedding. Nothing camp. A "legitimate" marriage for his relatives. But he was never gonna force me. It had to be my idea too. Chances were extremely likely I was gonna outlive him, so I'd be doing most of the raising. And I admit, I was vehemently against it at first. Vehemently. Vocally vehement. But he didn't mind. I had a right to an opinion, and he was happy to have me. And I'm happy to have him.

But I changed my mind, didn't I? Maybe because I never liked being the one stopping someone else from getting what they want. Or maybe it's because I respected my husband's sincerity, his consideration. It's one of the many reasons I fell in love with him.

After a few years, we finally got the OK from the adoption agency to bring Quentin home. He's only four. Great big smile. Red hair. Infectious laugh. It's been strange having him around the house these past two weeks. Like a house guest that won't go away. Because it's his home now too. He's our son. *My* son. Holy hell, I'm still getting used to that.

Something amazing happened today, a scene I know I'm gonna remember on my deathbed. My husband and I spent the afternoon playing little Quentin to death, tickle-fighting him into a pile of giggles, before my husband had to get back to work. While he was in the office, I was holding Quentin by the window in my favorite chair. It was raining outside, that typical Danvers downpour, and I was cradling sleepy Quentin against my chest, rocking him slowly, soft rain tapping on the windowpane, that gray foggy overcast backlit by buried sun. And I was singing "Levon" like a hushed little lullaby, smiling down at the little man sleeping so sweetly against my chest. It was just him and I in that moment. Me and my son. And I felt such a warm feeling enter me, enough to make my voice waver as I sang.

I laid Quentin down to sleep just a moment ago. Tucked him in. Kissed his cheek. And I stood a little bit by his bedside, smiling some more. I decided there and then what I needed to do, what my duty was. Quentin's my son now. He's not getting tossed aside again. We're not his birth parents, those little baby-faced Gen Zs too horny and stupid to understand husbandry. He's not gonna be ignored or underestimated the way my parents ignored and underestimated me. He'll be raised right. With love of this world. The real world. IRL.

My friends from high school, those social media addicts, anxiety-plagued children themselves, raising progeny of their own because they feel they have to, give their spawn tablets and phones with data to keep them busy, to keep them quiet, because it's just too damn hard otherwise. But they'll wonder what went wrong one day, won't they? Not me. Quentin will not end up like that. He'll be better. A great man with the right values, the right priorities, the right worldview. That's what will make him so great. So strong. So important. So influential.

If I have to have a son, so be it. But he's gonna be *my* son.

1.

manifesto

Quentin will touch grass. He'll breathe air. He'll mess in the dirt, in the sand, in the rain. He'll learn to be sad, to be bored, to be the generator of his own happiness. And as he grows, he'll learn his place in the world, what world his Zaddy grew up in, what world his Daddy grew up in, so he'll have a complete societal timeline, essential context he'll only thank us for. In that regard, we're perfect parents for little Quentin. His Daddy, born in 1964, is on the cusp of Baby Boomer and Gen X, a subset few people know already has a name, Generation Jones (i.e. "keeping up with the Joneses"), and I was born in 1995, making me a Zillennial, too young to remember the 90s but old enough to remember a world before the Internet. Quentin having two dads is already such a good thing, a perfect introduction for a little boy to understand a world without gender norms or societal expectations, but we're also demographic outsiders as well. We forged our own identity, not relying on age-related stereotypes or stupid generational hive-mind to guide us.

As the world changes, we'll have to adjust Quentin's upbringing. When movie theaters, Broadway shows and live concerts start fading away due to rising ticket prices, we'll invest the time and money to bring him physically wherever, simultaneously educating him on what the world was taking away from him, how great such a "luxury" used to be when it was simply the norm, easily affordable for everyone. And as the labor strikes keep getting worse, each one greedier than the one before, and the student loan crisis getting so bad that a general bailout would single-handedly bankrupt the average taxpayer, and most if not all blue-collar jobs getting replaced by AI, Quentin will be aware of it all.

Of course the economy will keep getting worse as Quentin ages, more inflation followed by another Great Recession. And when the Millennials finally get into power, the generation that practically invented cold, dispassionate streamlining, America will suddenly see the scientific and economic benefits of purely virtual education. No angry taxpayers bitching about how expensive facilities are, property taxes and energy costs always on the rise. Everything can simply be so digital and intimate and *green*, not to mention their kids won't miss a single day of school due to inclement weather, nor will they waste an hour or two on recess, the place where kids either get bullied or get into trouble. And AI can analyze the details of each individual student, quantifying statistics of attention, focus, and probability of potential for the next generation of teachers, guaranteeing that no child will get left behind. And all while saving millions of tax dollars a year?

It'll start in the colleges, all in the name of saving students from their loans, before it trickles down to the high schools by the time Quentin is six years old, then to the middle school level by the time he's twelve. But I won't let him do the virtual thing. I'll ignore the statistics confirming no long-term degradation of social skills, because how can they know if there's no long-term degradation of social skills if there aren't any social environments left to monitor? No way. Daddy and I will just have to homeschool him. In-person learning. Recess. No screens in his face or cameras in his eyes. No feeling of constantly being watched or monitored. A pressure-free environment. Oh, and when Quentin asks why he can't go to school with other kids, the way I did growing up, the way Daddy did growing up, I'll remind him that the alternative, what the stupid Department of Education considers "real" middle school, is just him in his room, plugged into a computer with no real classmates, just pictures of them, moving pictures, GIF thumbnails in a way. And when Quentin asks why the other parents aren't homeschooling their kids, I'll have to be honest with him and explain that they just don't care about their kids' mental health the way I do for Quentin's, that they would rather things stay just as they are. And I'll tell Quentin this: if he feels isolated or weird now, know that at least he's being raised right. That will only work out for him in the end.

By the time Quentin hits puberty, my cute little redhead will suddenly be an assertive young man, a bushy shaggy mess of red curls with a huge nose, freckles, long lanky bones, no muscle on him (no matter how hard he tries) and a perpetual frown (no matter how hard he tries). By then he won't have to be told to stay off technology; he'll want to on his own. He'll ask Daddy and I to teach him how to drive, for real — something completely unheard of thanks to all the self-driving cars, most Gen A inherently not knowing how to drive — because knowing how to drive is the right way to be. And when Daddy and I finally allow him to get a cell phone at the age of sixteen, he'll insist on having one without data, simply a phone without a computer, because having an unnetworked cell phone is the right way to be.

And whenever he does go on the computer, he'll do so as a general observer, full of curiosity and critical thinking, browsing social media but never actively participating, reading up on Wikipedia to fill in the gaps on what had been, confirming what we always told him, that the old world faded away only a few decades ago, and yet it was completely gone. He'll only want to listen to older music, his fathers' tastes, 60s, 70s and 80s music with select aughts and 10s exceptions, but never anything new. Only real music with real instruments and real personality behind it. He'll only watch movies on Blu-Ray, never streaming. He'll only read books with pages and spines, not e-ink. He'll insist on learning how to actually sign his name, in cursive, using a pen. And he won't feel a void when it comes to not having friends. Because he'll have nothing in common with those fools with big IQs and no social skills, no reverence, just ADHD, depression and anxiety, hopping from short-term trend to short-term trend, wondering in vain why nothing seemed to really stick.

Every once in a while, Quentin will pity his peers, his Gen A brethren, for seemingly getting worse and worse. A bile will form in his throat as the years go by, that gap between the ideal past and fickle present growing and irrevocably deepening. Then a new form of depression will develop inside Quentin, the kind old men seem to get: the decay of a once-great thing, unstoppable and irreversible.

And just when he'll need his dads to help him put faith back in humanity, his Daddy will have a bad fall. He'll suddenly need daily care, care I will provide with my entire being, which means I won't have time to homeschool Quentin anymore. I'd have no choice but to send him to a private high school, an in-person institution, one of the last in the state. I'm sure Quentin would do fine in a place like that, his independence having been a priority from the start. He could solve his own boredom, generate his own happiness, his own value, just around the time his peers discover how much of childhood was a padded cell, adulthood a wide-open space, a revelation they'll react to with fear and immaturity, pleading to go back in. But not Quentin. He'll finally be allowed to be the adult he's always wanted to be, celebrated for his maturity instead of being mocked for it, valued for his critical thinking instead of marginalized.

And he'll go to Emerson College, his Zaddy's *alma mater*, surrounded by all those ambitious Gen Alphas, those "Children of COVID" as the Millennials will disparagingly call them by then, those other old souls that prefer in-person learning and critical thinking, desperate to change the world, to be greater.

But Quentin will endure a hard awakening upon graduation. He didn't want to be friends with morons, because who'd want to be friends with morons? Well, turns out, everyone. Every other Gen A, so digitally absorbed, so consumed with advertising and sensationalism, will have a digital paper trail just as old as they are. Suzie Q the Insta addict, having used the same account since she was four, will have 35 million followers by the time she graduates college, helping her stand out on paper enough to land a high-profile job right out of school. By comparison, who'd wanna hire Quentin Wagner, that bleeding heart nostalgist, that quirky 70s aficionado with no followers, no likes, no data fed into any algorithm anywhere, when they could just hire one of the ten millions of others that did all that and so much more?

Quentin won't understand at first, but he will. His screenwriting career will be dead in the water, his once flaming optimism dwindling year after year, until the day he wakes up

in a shitty Worcester apartment, only a few hours away from
his dinner shift at that shitty diner he works at, only to realize
he's twenty-seven. Five years out of college with nothing to
show for it. And he'll feel so alone. So ignored. A total failure.
Like he didn't even matter. Like *nothing* even mattered. Not
even him being right.

Quentin will schedule his suicide for July 21, 2046. A Saturday. Great day to go out on. Before then he'll have to get a
gun. Something small. A nice pistol perhaps. Semi-automatic.
Nothing like *The Deer Hunter* with a spinning chamber and
lots of clicking. Fuck no. Something simple. Almost plastic
looking. Oh, and he'll have to go get a bottle of Jack too. And
fuck it, cocaine. He'll have a nice little celebration of life beforehand. A good record playing. Maybe a movie or two. And
then when it's all done, he'll blow his brains out and finally
leave that shitty decaying world of his. And no last goodbyes
to Zaddy. He'll probably be too busy to answer as always. Already bad enough he had to deal with all of Daddy's medical
drama; Quentin won't dump his shit on top too. And what if
he let slip what he had planned? What if he changed his mind?
He can't have that. It's already on the calendar. He already decided to do it.

When July 21, 2046 finally arrives, his last day on Earth,
Quentin will find himself surprisingly calm. A strange sense
of closure throughout. Like a good riddance to it all. A sense
of control. And he'll go about his day as he meant to. A visit
to his favorite park. A triple scoop of ice cream. A humble final
dinner to go with his Jack and coke. But as he plays that favorite album of his, Led Zeppelin's untitled fourth album, that last
track on Side 2 getting closer and closer, Quentin will slip into
a total emotional breakdown, the graceful *coup de grâce* he en-
visioned turning into a desperate, dark, painful downfall of

despair. He'll cry. Wail. Grab the gun early and put it to his temple only to learn (CLICK!) it wasn't loaded. That'll fuck him up more. He'll smash his face in the mirror. Fall to the floor, landing on his hand, breaking two fingers in the process. And he'll throw up on the toilet lid, passing out on the bathroom floor.

Quentin will drive himself to the hospital the next day to fix his face and right hand, all that natural daylight and random people mulling about hitting him in a new way, giving him chills. He won't be able to process what it is he's feeling until he's in the ER waiting room, sitting next to that ten-year-old watching *Seinfeld* of all things on his mother's tablet. Quentin's favorite show. What are the chances of that? But the kid won't be laughing, not even a smile. Because the studio audience did all the laughing for him. And that moment will shake Quentin's soul. What a poor kid. So devoid of emotion. Stunted even. What Quentin just went through was a devastating, dreadful experience, and yet no one could say it wasn't unequivocally *his*. His pain hadn't been approved by a corporate focus group. His reactions hadn't been fed through a hyper-intelligent algorithm, rewarding him with a curated advertisement. He healed himself by living, not memes. THAT was what his Zaddy raised him to handle. THAT was real life. It might've been ugly and awful, but it was fucking his. All his and no one else's. That kid had no idea how much better life could be if he was the one doing the laughing, the one doing the thinking. All he had to do was look up. Look around and live. But no one thought like that, did they? That was the problem.

No way, Quentin will tell himself, waiting for the nurse to come back to that second, smaller waiting room. He can't be the only one. Someone else had to see it too. There's ten billion people in the world, goddamnit. All he needed was one, someone that wasn't his Zaddy who got it too. Just one.

When Quentin gets home, he'll look at his laptop and bitterly realize what he had to do, the very thing he swore never to do. By 2046, "everyone" will be on TrueSwitch, a Frankenstein fusion of Reddit and TikTok. If he simply created an account, even for just a little bit, and posted something, millions of people will see it, his words shoved in their faces against their will. And for the tiniest of moments, Quentin will be glad such a rude violation exists. But with the cold control of a scientist, he'll experiment with this thing, this thing he never let in, swearing it'll never corrupt him. It's just research. Yes, that's what it is. Research for his next screenplay.

Quentin will half-ass his profile, click Create Post, and let it all out:

Before the Internet, the world was a true ecosystem. When something drastic happened, people reacted. Most times one camp reacted stronger than another, sure, but it was still a true, genuine reaction. Society had to adapt in order to compensate. It never matched 100%, but it was closer than it was before, a true compromise, even if admittedly watered down from the original's intended ideal. And so had it been for decades and decades. The Greatest Generation had World War II and memories of the Depression. The Silent Gen had Communism and Korea. The Baby Boomers had Vietnam, feminism, gay rights, Black rights, rights on rights on rights. Gen X had MTV and cubicles. The Millennials had it all, the Internet, until the world turned upside down. Even Gen Z had something of their own: TikTok dances. That and the almighty algorithm.

But what about us? What do we get? Scraps? Not even. We get memories of scraps. Nothing is our own.

Think about it, how much of what we see is ours? Not "made ours," actually ours? AI doesn't create, it repackages. Covers and remakes cover and remake what was once new, original and fresh. There used to be fresh, you know. There used to be new. There used to be original.

But no one reacts genuinely anymore. Everything's all muddled. Our senses discombobulated. Our intuitions muted. We second-guess ourselves, told by the world — the world of the Internet, that is — that our happiness isn't actually happiness, that it's simply naiveté. And anger. That's not anger, that's just what they want you to feel. It means someone's manipulating you. Oh, that safety and satisfaction you're feeling? That's just you letting everyone down, complacency, you looking the other way instead of powering through. And that fear of the unknown? That's just plain old bigotry. Don't bother hoping. That's too unrealistic. Dreaming is for stupid people.

Who can grow in an environment like that? No one. In fact, we're going backwards because of it. We double down, root in. And as time goes by, we wonder why it's not getting any better. But how can it, when greedy corporations own our phones and our screens and our Wi-Fi, when social media uses algorithms and trick psychology to keep us addicted to stale echo chambers? We're netting zero because they want us to, because it keeps us predictable, and maximum predictability equals maximum profit. They exploit our fears, our insecurities, our weakness, because it's good business. That's America in a nutshell, ain't it? Good business?

They trick us into giving them our data, gaslighting us into forgetting that privacy is actually okay (and kinda normal), and then they take that data and sell it to the highest bidder. They don't even tell us, they just do it. And news, honest news, regulated journalism, you can only find behind a paywall.

Otherwise you get lies, lies for free. No wonder no one knows what the hell's going on.

Not to mention we don't even think it's strange anymore that corporations sell us microphones to eavesdrop on us, using our kitchen conversations to fuel the ads we see. We don't think it's weird when we go into a grocery store and a computer uses the data off our phones to average out the demographic of its current customer population so it can play the music most of us statistically would like to hear, keeping us in there as long and as happy as possible. We don't think it's odd that our phones store our credit card information for vendors to auto-charge us anytime they want so they don't have to pay for cashiers and cut down on theft, all in the name of "convenience." Why is all that normal to us?

Because it's how it's always been.

We don't care anymore because the Internet gives us everything we want. If we forget a celebrity's age, we just hop onto Wikipedia and find out in two seconds. All the music, movies, TV, theater, YouTube videos and porn that have ever existed is sitting in our pocket. Our economy literally needs the Internet to survive. Most of us work from home. Our parents create content to pay the bills. It's how we get our news. How we talk to people. Concerts. Documentaries. Education. We use it to process the real world. And it tells us what car to buy, what paper towels work better than others, which president isn't trying to fuck us. But I ask you this: Why?

Why is the Internet so ingrained in our lives? Why are our phones capable of Wi-Fi and Dropbox and Bluetooth, with calendars and clocks and everything else? Why do they have cameras and microphones? Why do we need to look at it first thing in the morning? Why do we seem to live more by documenting our lives through selfies and videos? Why do we keep using social media despite knowing how it hurts us doing so, how much harder it makes our lives, even though we hate their shady practices and greedy marketing, knowing very well how cancerous they've become? Why do we keep feeding algorithms despite knowing how unethical they are? Why are we shocked by our own passivity, our absolutism? Why are we so starved for love? Why? Because it always was this way? Because our parents did the same thing? Since when did that stop us?

Our parents, the Millennials, became addicted to that digital world, so they felt it was only natural to pass that addiction on to their kids. But we're the only ones paying that debt. We feel like our lives can only be real if our phones have 16K resolution, at least until 32K comes out. We prioritize Internet bills over our life savings and wonder why we can't afford a house by thirty. We binge a new TV show in the span of a week, just because we can, and wonder why we forget about it three months later. Even our choices aren't real. They're just our parents' choices. It is them, not us, controlling the trends of the algorithm. We complain about everything being unoriginal and yet shoot down anything that makes us feel strange. You know what that is, that feeling? Difference. Difference is natural. It's how we grow. But the Internet doesn't understand difference. It only matches. Its products are bland because we're bland. We never used to be, but we certainly are now.

All the brilliance of the real world, that fringe analog struggling to outlive a digital world, was destroyed by a generation of spoiled, stuck-up dope fiends. Is that fair? Should our lives be enslaved to a machine that isn't even our own? Don't we have any choices left? How can any of this be legal? How can anyone call it ethical?

You know why it's legal? Because we let it happen. It's ethical because we don't believe or care about nuance anymore.

Our choices are as such: like or dislike, share or block, post or delete, tag or ignore.

Don't any of you want to live? Haven't you had enough of this bullshit? Don't your eyes hurt? Is the brightness too high? Okay. Great. Take a break. Unplug. Log out. Unsubscribe. Power down. Go offline.

And stay there.

Why not? There's so much out there, so much to do. But I get it. How else would you get your news? How else are you gonna make friends? What about your favorite shows and music? Yes, such a transition would be very rough. But the Internet is a prison, a cancer of absolutism and algorithms, of vanity and shame. Corporations use it to warp our opinions. The articles we read are view dependent. Headlines intentionally exploit our anger and hate for maximum exposure. They lie all the time, manufacturing outrage over petty things, encouraging us to cancel people for things they declare to be irrelevant or potentially harmful. Our smartphones, our voice assistants, our geotrackers, our search history, are used against us, simply data for companies to predict our minds with horrifying accuracy. No one regulates what they can't do. They have free rein because we let them, so stop letting them. Stop giving them their views. Stop sharing your life with them. There was once a world without them for thousands of years. They had their time.

We have the power to kill them. We have the power to let them go. To undo everything.

We know what we want, not them. We never asked to pay their debt. We don't want to be like them. We don't want them calling us "Children of COVID" anymore. We want to be better than that. We want to be the generation that woke up. The one that decided one day: "I want to live!"

So let's do it. Let's live. Let's do the impossible. Let's make our own choices. Let's write our own fucking algorithm.

#Unplug

Quentin will hit post without rereading and close his laptop. And he'll sit on those words buzzing around his head, those angry words, and he'll tell himself to forget it, to move on. But against his better judgment, he'll reopen the lid and reread that masterpiece... only to feel disgusted. What the fuck was all that? How could such incoherent drivel actually start off as an actual philosophical statement before falling off a cliff into an inconsistent mess of anarcho-communist sentiment and clichéd classist melodrama? No wonder everyone sounds stupid on social media. It all just came pouring out of him. And it's so goddamn cringy. Like something a hormonal teenager would come up with. So beneath him. So far under his caliber. And all those words! How can so many words mean so little?

As embarrassed as Quentin will be with that impulsive anti-establishment word vomit, he'll feel such nonsense not even worth the effort or the time it would take to delete it. He'll simply delete the app instead. He won't let himself become an active TrueSwitch user, dependent on content every day, dependent on a place to vent bullshit to an audience of none. That won't be an option for him. He won't allow it to be. Because he's so much better than everyone else.

But before he goes to sleep, Quentin will find himself smiling a little bit. Even if no one heard it, even if it's buried under millions of others happening every day, every hour, Quentin managed to make a tree fall in the middle of the forest. A virtual sequoia is lying on its side somewhere because of him. An actual dent in this world. That's actually more than nothing, isn't it? No wonder everyone's so addicted.

But Quentin will have no idea just how efficient the TrueSwitch algorithm is. Not only does it use a user's past engagement on TrueSwitch itself, but thanks to some clever legislative trickery, it also uses every other social media network the user has ever used. The goal of such a monstrous breach of ethics is to induce a sort of surprise in new TrueSwitch users at how amazing it is at replicating their exact niche right off the bat. It'll be that surprise, that one-two punch, that'll make TrueSwitch the top dog social network for Generation Alpha.

But because Quentin's digital footprint is quite literally zero, TrueSwitch will have no data of his to work with. That lack of specificity will have to be made up for in other ways. Using the most powerful AI in the world, TrueSwitch's algorithm will (in the span of a second) analyze the language of Quentin's post, taking note of its general tone, sentence structure, complex vocabulary, lack of contractions, main idea, etc., to determine its ideal target audience.

The general rule of thumb will be as follows: the more wholesome and cordial the opinion, the less likely it'll be seen organically, due to the lack of potential engagement. Conversely, the harsher and more abrasive the opinion, the more visibility it will receive, due to the extremely high potential of engagement.

In mere seconds, despite nothing to go on except Quentin's fiery verbiage, TrueSwitch will determine his post's ideal audience to be the following:

(A) The top 25% of TrueSwitch's most active users.

(B) The users it considers more likely to engage with critical thinking posts.

(C) The users it considers more likely to share rather than comment or like.

Thanks to TrueSwitch's algorithm being so damn good at its job, 750 million people will read Quentin's post over the next thirty days.

2.

viral

One of the first people to share Quentin's post, no doubt an essential reason for its virality, will be Jax Halsteder from Nekoosa, Wisconsin. Nineteen years old. Noticeably unattractive. Tiny balding head. Heavy body. Disproportionate torso. A pink splotchy birthmark on his neck and pock marks on his cheeks. Cyberbullied since he was four. His mom ran out on him years ago, before Jax could remember her. His father will lose his trucker job soon after, because a human being operating a vehicle is so obviously an expensive luxury when a simple nav computer could do it for free. And so Jax's dad will drink and hit, drink and hit, to toughen the piece of shit up (and to make up for his own unfortunate failure of a life, but mostly the former, because Jesus, *look at him!*). And Jax will be forced to internalize his pain, that feeling of constant unwantedness, choosing instead to devout his life to coding, literally the most in-demand job in America by 2046, even more than doctors. And his determination to outsmart those asshole jocks and fickle sluts by actually having a brain, let alone a usable skill, will earn him a full-ride Software Engineering scholarship to MIT. It's like he won the lottery, fighting his way out of Nekoosa, finally a chance at a new life. But when he gets to Cambridge, finally surrounded by other brainiacs in physical spaces, Jax will discover a new flavor of unwantedness: impostor syndrome. His talent wasn't what got him the scholarship; it was his shitty circumstances. He was the token yokel and everyone knew it.

Jax will stumble upon Quentin's post expecting to mock it, but to his surprise it'll strike a chord. This Quentin guy had a point. Their society *did* used to be better, more accessible, until Millennials like his dad fucked it up for everyone. Jax will share Quentin's post and sit back, dwelling on it some more, and he'll realize how much he agreed with Quentin's philosophy. How much he's always agreed with it.

A few days later, Esabell Cortina-Gomez will hear about Quentin's post through some friends. Twenty years old. Black hair. Clean face. Olive skin. Sweet little voice with lots of spunk. Confident posture. She lived in California her whole life before starting her Public Relations and Marketing double major at Boston's Northeastern University. Her parents, Javier Cortina and Elizabeth Gomez, were two prominent civil rights activists in their time. Speaking out during #MeToo and #BlackLivesMatter. Attending anti-Trump rallies and *Roe v. Wade* marches. Throwing bricks at pigs during the George Floyd protests. Making sure to always stay aware. To always have a phone on hand. To speak out. Elevate. Educate. Fighting hard to undo institutional damage. To try and make the world a better place. But they had to reroute their priorities when Esabell came along, shifting toward digital advertising, making sure to raise their daughter with stories of their exploits so she'll have the same fire they used to have before the condom broke.

Upon reading Quentin's post, Esabell will finally understand what her parents meant by "stay woke." She had been complacent. Complacent in something BAD. Now she has a chance to follow in her parents' footsteps. To be part of a cause in its early days. To fix the world like they did.

Around this time, in South Bend, Indiana, Amphibian Cantell (Phibs for short) will discover Quentin's post. Twenty-three years old. 5-foot-6. Big glasses. Lips like a beak. Massive hands. Crystal-blue eyes. His parents, content creators working from home, too burnt out from all the problems in the world — the injustices, the rising prices, the wasted hope, the scary wars and slaughters going on in the Outernet, the late stage of their capitalism, the corruption on every fucking level, the futility of anything getting better anytime soon, constantly getting barraged by negativity every time they turned on the news or looked at their phones or looked out the window or read the comments of their videos — haven't been able to do anything of value because of it, least of all raise their son. It was all just too much for them. So Phibs learned he had to settle for a lonely life, always needing more attention than he could possibly get, having no strength in him to go out and do his own thing.

But when Phibs reads Quentin's post, it'll all suddenly make sense. The damaging effect the Internet had on his own parents. How they passed that damage onto himself. And for the first time in his life, Phibs will be filled with a drive, a passion, a determination, a strength he will want to define him. And he'll want to find that mastermind, that genius that gave him this new feeling he loved so much, but he'll come up short. No last name in his profile. No email attached. No phone number. Just "Quentin." But Phibs won't let that stop him. He'll have to get creative.

Jaymeigh Grady-Smith-Waterhouse-Price, a twenty-two-year-old Political Science major at UC Berkeley, will finally hear of Quentin's TrueSwitch post two weeks later than seemingly everyone else. Long black hair. Pale plain face. Chronically offline and proud of it. She'll be lying out on Santa Monica sand, on summer break, reading Dostoevsky for fun, when a girlfriend of hers, Ghiuliyette Wintergrass (pronounced "Juliet"), will spot her on the beach and call out, waving hi, strolling over to chit-chat. Among other things Ghiuliyette will casually mention #Unplug, going off on some tangent regarding her own Internet obsession and how she really needs to cut it down going forward. And Jaymeigh won't instantly know what she's talking about, prompting Ghiuliyette to go, "You've never heard of #Unplug?!" in that tone Jaymeigh's heard far too many times before. And Jaymeigh will deny it all with a hint of annoyance, because she doesn't care about the latest Internet fads. But Ghiuliyette will aggressively shove Quentin's post in her face anyway, and despite herself Jaymeigh will actually read it. But Jaymeigh still won't care one iota about #Unplug, even *after* reading it, and Ghiuliyette will furiously walk away with a pleasant smile, secretly resenting Jaymeigh for being a stuck-up bitch, reading a dumbass book drier than the sand she's lying on, wondering why she's even friends with her.

But Jaymeigh will shrug off all judgment toward Ghiuliyette. As emotional and stupid as that TrueSwitch post was, Ghiuliyette has every right to obsess over it, just as Jaymeigh had every right to obsess over Dostoevsky.

On August 23, 2046, more than a month since he attempted suicide, Quentin will clock out of the diner and head out to his car, but before he'll get the chance to open the door and climb in, he'll get a call from an unknown number with a strange area code. Too curious to reject it, Quentin will swipe, leaning a shoulder against his driver's-side door. "Hello?"

"Quentin?" a young man will ask.

Quentin will furrow his brow.

"This *is* Quentin, isn't it?!" the voice will exclaim. "Oh my God! I can't believe it! I finally found you!"

"Huh?"

"I'm sorry. The name's Phibs. I just wanted to be able to thank you for what you wrote. It literally changed my life."

Quentin will drop his keys at that. He'll bend over to pick it up. "What do you mean? What did I write?"

"Your post on TrueSwitch."

Quentin will chuckle with flattery and confusion. "Oh, uh... How did you get this number?"

"Your website."

"My website? I took that down years ago."

"I found an old Wayback of it. It was a pain in the ass, believe me, but I found it!"

Quentin's stomach will turn. "Hold on a second." He'll put the call on speaker and redownload the app as Phibs drones on lengthily about his deep dive into all things Quentin using the few starting points he could publicly access, tantamount to using wooden sticks to create a lightning bolt. And when Quentin reopens TrueSwitch, his eyes will widen at the sight of his DMs in the quadruple digits, red dots all over the interface and those three little lines in the top left corner. His post, that little bit of vomit, had been TrueSwitch's most liked post of all time for over a month now.

Quentin will brace for the worst when he taps that DM inbox, shocked again to see messages solely of support. Complete strangers, thousands of little voices, all in agreement that something should be done about the Internet, that it was a bad idea from the start, that someone really needs to undo it for all their sakes. Especially noticeable will be a message from a woman named Esabell inviting him personally to speak at Northeastern University sometime that Fall. Apparently he's got a huge following there, and they're all desperate to hear from the man himself.

In the face of all that validation, that rush of support for an opinion he truly thought he was alone in having, Quentin will actually burst into tears.

3.

coalition

Quentin will first meet Amphibian Cantell outside Boston's Logan International Airport two days later, and they'll stop by the Esplanade to sit and talk about #Unplug. The first thing Quentin will notice about Phibs, besides his surprisingly persistent enthusiasm, will be how naturally anti-social he is. Awkward lack of eye contact. Quiet speaking voice. The occasional $10 word choice, obviously meant to impress, only to come off as obtuse. During their conversation, Quentin will reveal his own inexperience with the Internet, let alone a "philosophy" as Phibs keeps calling it, claiming his post to be nothing particularly special or unique, just how he felt about the whole thing. And Phibs will suggest, as a way to move forward, that they meet with the colleges in Boston that most gravitated to Quentin's "manifesto" and discuss as a group the best way to implement #Unplug on a larger scale. Feeling he has nothing to lose, Quentin will agree to one meeting.

Going through Quentin's TrueSwitch metrics, Phibs will narrow down the post's largest response to three Boston campuses: Northeastern University, Quentin's own Emerson College, and (strangely enough) MIT. Phibs will then contact

Esabell Cortina-Gomez, that woman from Northeastern that DM'd Quentin, and negotiate on Quentin's behalf a neutral place for the three colleges to meet. Phibs and Esabell will then spread word across the three campuses for them to meet Quentin at the NonProfit Center on South Street on Friday, September 7 at 8 PM.

Two hundred people will show up for that first meeting. As uncomfortable as it'll be for the attendees, being so cramped among all those real-life people, it'll be even stranger for Quentin himself. All those students actually made the journey from their campuses to South Street, all in the name of that goofy philosophy of his. When it's time for Quentin to speak, he'll find himself struck dumb for a moment before going off on the one thing he hates more than anything, the Internet, how much better America was (and the world) before its widespread implementation. When he reaches a logical roadblock, pausing with no second topic to transition to, Esabell will thankfully take over, talking into her own mic about her own contentious relationship with the Internet, following it with an offer to let someone else tell their story, someone in the audience.

Phibs will then relay the microphone to the first volunteer: an MIT sophomore named Jax Halsteder. He'll start off strong, going on and on about coding and how he once saw it as valuable to society, only to realize how wrong he was thanks to Quentin's post. He'll end his testimony with a loud declaration that he had dropped out of his Software Engineering program just before their meeting tonight, thus forfeiting his full-ride scholarship to MIT. This will incur a loud applause from the attendees, but Quentin will be downright gobsmacked by it. For the first time he'll understand just how much of a nuclear bomb his post was. If someone walked down the street and bumped into Jax, telling him to quit school and forfeit that scholarship of his, the one he fought so hard to earn, there's no way he'd do it. But a social media post "showing up" on his feed, allowing Jax to "discover" it, was enough to plant that very seed in his brain. Just because it showed up on his phone. Just because it was text and not someone's voice. It slipped right into his world and completely redirected his life. With all of his being, Quentin will want to scold Jax for doing such a stupid thing over a fucking TrueSwitch post, but he'll stay quiet, reminding himself how impulsive he was when he was nineteen, all those years ago.

As the meeting goes on, a loose consensus will form among the party: an official movement established by the three schools, a coalition that will organize a formal nationwide boycott of all digital enterprises, replacing them with the analog solutions that will cause the least amount of damage and disruption to an everyday person's life.

Before adjourning, Esabell will suggest they vote for representatives, one from each college, to form the governing body of their organization. The attendees from Emerson College will unanimously vote for Quentin Wagner, even though he wasn't a student there anymore. Northeastern will predictably pick Esabell as their representative, but when it's MIT's turn, they'll vote enthusiastically for Jax Halsteder. Jax will be moved beyond comprehension by such rallying support from his former brethren, something he had never experienced before. And Quentin will decipher that expression playing out on Jax's face, realizing they weren't so different after all.

The Coalition, now calling themselves the Unplug Movement, will meet again at the NonProfit Center the following Friday to openly discuss the terms of their official charter, a hundred or so new attendees joining them. For the next three hours, Quentin, Esabell and Jax will lead an open debate on the nuances of Unplug, its internal hierarchy, the relationship between Quentin's TrueSwitch post (now deemed "The Manifesto") and the newly established Unplug Movement, the logistics of an official nationwide boycott, and what should and should not be allowed in a post-Unplug world. Phibs, acting as Quentin's personal secretary, will summarize their agreed stances on a whiteboard. Despite such a potentially unstable town hall format, this second meeting will be executed with phenomenal politeness and decorum. Never at any time will self-censoring or chastisement feel necessary.

At the end of the third hour, Phibs will draft up the official Unplug Movement charter:

Quentin Wagner's TrueSwitch post ("Manifesto") shall henceforth serve as the symbolic spirit of the Unplug Movement, and can be adequately summarized through the following three tenants: (1) The creation of all digital-only spaces has been a colossal, catastrophic mistake, pushing back the creative and spiritual progress of humanity beyond all recognition. (2) Said digital-only spaces, being solely controlled by Millennials, seek only to advance Millennial priorities, and any economic, emotional, social, cultural, or journalistic value to be gained through the continued use of said digital-only spaces can only be done so at the significant physical, mental, emotional, financial and social detriment of Generation Alpha ("Gen A"). (3) Gen A, being the target demographic of said digital-only spaces, must be kept in a submissive, accepting position of complacency in order for said digital-only spaces to function as intended.

Therefore, because of the reasons highlighted above, a total nationwide boycott of all digital-only spaces is the most effective method of resistance. The Official Unplug Movement Boycott ("Boycott") will begin on January 1, 2047 at 12:00 AM EST with no intended end date. Implementation of the Boycott requires all Unplug Movement members to completely cease all use and financial contribution toward the following industries ("The Hateful Eight"): (1) e-commerce retail and their associated delivery mechanisms, (2) streaming services, (3) personalized and/or ad-driven search engines, (4) social media networks, including all digital social spaces, dating/hookup apps, networked video game lobbies, MMORPGs and any other metaversal realms, (5) networked electronic devices (tablets, smartphones, etc.), (6) pay-per-month subscriptions to digital products and software, (7) Internet Service Providers, cloud services, server farms, hardware manufacturing and software manufacturing, (8) automated driving cars, including hybrids with their Autopilot setting turned on.

During the Boycott, the following declining analog industries must be fully supported as official replacements of the Hateful Eight: department stores, specialty retail suppliers, shopping malls, record stores, movie theaters, live music venues, concert halls, restaurants, bars, nightclubs, local parks, hiking trails, sports complexes, bookstores, libraries, the United States Postal Service, home media rental stores, in-person houses of worship, and any other businesses or industries that have been driven toward bankruptcy due to the rise and/or dominance of digital alternatives.

The Official Unplug Email Newsletter ("Newsletter") shall be established immediately and serve the following purposes: (1) To inform all members of the internal affairs and progress reports of the Unplug Movement. (2) To serve as a free-access alternative to paid U.S. and World News services controlled by the Hateful Eight. (3) To provide said national and international news without bias or political filter. (4) To monitor the membership numbers of the Unplug Movement nationwide through the collection of email addresses.

The Coalition of the Unplug Movement ("Coalition") will operate as follows: The main headquarters will be established at Emerson College, headed by its representative Quentin Wagner, serving all administrative duties, including statements to the press and full-time operation of the Newsletter, prioritizing day-to-day functionality above all else. A second headquarters will be established at Northeastern University, headed by its representative Esabell Cortina-Gomez, serving all duties related to Unplug's public relations, marketing, branding and promotional efforts, prioritizing consistent reputation above all else. A third headquarters will be established at the Massachusetts Institute of Technology ("MIT"), headed by its representative Jax Halsteder, serving all duties regarding new member outreach, recruitment and official tally of membership totals, prioritizing continued growth and member satisfaction above all else.

On the first and third Fridays of every month, the three Coalition representatives will meet in the basement of Park Street Church to discuss biweekly updates, voting if necessary on future endeavors. Each representative is granted with the authority of their college's vote. A fourth non-partisan vote will be cast by Amphibian "Phibs" Cantell, unanimously designated to represent the Coalition itself. A three-fourths majority is required for all votes to pass.

Any additions to this charter must be approved through a biweekly Coalition meeting vote or during an emergency Coalition gathering.

One by one, the attendees of the Unplug Movement's inaugural meeting will step up to the table and sign the charter. Some confusion will be made at first as to how they're supposed to sign a piece of paper, everything legally binding to their knowledge being either a thumbprint scan or an NIST-DSS e-sig. Quentin will have to demonstrate for the Coalition the way everyone used to sign documents back in the day, a strange sloppiness called "cursive." Rather than be intimidated by such a messy, unusual way to write one's name, the Coalition will instead be ecstatic at the foreign nature of it all, feeling like they're living in the future already.

As everyone files out of the conference center, Jax will stay behind to tenderly approach Quentin for the first time. "I'm really excited about all this," he'll say with a big smile.

Quentin will nod, smiling as well, suddenly feeling like an authority figure. "I am too."

Jax will awkwardly fidget in place, the echo of that empty conference room actually freaking him out. "I really should've said something before, but..."

"What?"

"Maybe I should wait."

"It's okay," Quentin will insist with assurance. "Tell me."

Jax will soften at that. "Why an *email* newsletter? I thought the idea was to get off the Internet."

"There's no exploitation in emails. No ad space. No data sales."

"Yeah, but the Hateful Eight will still be getting their money. People need to have Wi-Fi to get our newsletters."

Quentin will sigh harshly. "You're right. You really should've said something."

"I'm sorry."

"It's fine. You're not the only one." Quentin will scratch his forehead. "Problem is, I don't see another option."

"Why not a postal newsletter?"

Quentin will chuckle. "We're nowhere near that yet."

"What do you mean?"

"The cost of paper. Postage. Getting everyone's address. Securely storing everyone's address. Shipping speeds on a good day, let alone when they're understaffed, and that's even worse during peak holidays. And what if a whole bunch gets lost in transit? We'd have to rapid resend. You got the money for all that? I don't."

Jax will think for a second. "We can always charge for the newsletter."

"No way."

"Like a membership fee—"

"Then we'd be just like them!" Quentin will interrupt passionately. "Just another truth-behind-paywall model. The moment we start making money off our members, the whole thing's ruined. All we'd be thinking about is how to get more money out of 'em to pay for more things, and then who knows what'll happen." Quentin will shake his head. "No. If we want this thing to work, we gotta be like Wikipedia. Free and voluntary. It's the only way to avoid corruption."

Jax won't emote, on the outside at least. "But that's the Internet."

"It's Wikipedia. C'mon. Everyone loves Wikipedia."

Jax will chuckle nervously. "We can't idolize the Internet!"

"It's cheaper and faster!" Quentin will snap back. "I'm sorry, but pure analog's just too much of a luxury at the moment." He'll pause a moment to calm himself down. "It's not like the entire Internet's bad, you know. It has its good parts, like everything else."

Jax will furrow his brow. "Um..." He'll lean back on his heels, confused and a little hurt. "You... you are *joking*, right?"

Quentin will look at Jax's dumb face and realize he's actually super serious, truly not understanding the nuance of his
argument. He'll rapidly readjust, clearing his throat and
shrugging it off. "Yeah. Of course I'm joking. Of course. I'm
just bad at... Humor's not my thing. I'm sorry."

Jax will laugh off his relief. "Oh! Good!"

Quentin will rub the back of his head. "And as for your...
I suppose we can have a postal equivalent. There has to be a
way we can work it out."

"But what about the money?"

Quentin will hesitate again, really not wanting to say it.
"If people wanna throw us a donation or something, knowing
it would help us stay postal, that's fine. But it has to be optional. We're not forcing anyone. And we're not spending it
on anything besides postage and paper, agreed?"

Jax will grin. "Great. Night." He'll leave, shrugging off
Quentin's initial hesitation. It's been a long night. He probably
didn't mean it.

But Quentin will stay where he is on that stage, realizing
for the first time that following Phibs's advice and going
through the colleges might not have been the wisest decision.

4.

evening

In the weeks that follow, the Unplug Movement will run efficiently and succinctly with little to no problems. Jax will succeed in spreading word of the Unplug Movement to five other colleges in Boston. He'll even fly out to Los Angeles for a week to do some West Coast campaigning, focusing mainly on USC and UCLA. Quentin will be quite perturbed in having to pay such an unnecessary bill, especially considering they have a fucking hashtag for this very purpose, but Jax will continue to refuse to use the Internet, even for the greater good of unplugging those under its spell.

Esabell, meanwhile, will spend her time building a strong headquarters on Northeastern's campus, representing the Unplug Movement at several networking lunches for budding non-profits. She'll even take an extended leave of absence from her studies to prioritize her work with Unplug.

Quentin and Phibs, working out of Emerson College, will successfully start up the Unplug Newsletter, available via email and a postal equivalent, the two of them figuring out the best sources for them to cite as well as all the other kinks associated with writing a weekly periodical.

On Friday, November 2, 2046, during their fourth bi-weekly meetup, Esabell will announce an invitation she received for Quentin to appear on *The Evening Show* Monday the 19th, an offer they'd have to accept by day's end in order to be on the schedule.

Jax will instantly vote against it, reminding everyone that *The Evening Show*'s network is owned by the largest Internet Service Provider in the country, having owned it even before cable went the way of the dodo. The reason Roger Heffer is still its host is because he says exactly what his parent company wants him to say, and his invitation for Quentin to be on the show is not Roger catering to the new Gen A whim of the week, but a trap intended to mock and dismantle the Unplug Movement before it could properly begin.

Esabell, ever the optimist due to her wealthy, progressive upbringing, will openly doubt Jax's theory, reminding everyone that *The Evening Show* is the biggest and most watched late-night show on television because Roger even bothered to cater to Gen A, and Quentin being on the show would give the Boycott itself a massive boost of nationwide exposure.

Phibs, the neutral party representing the Coalition itself, will stay silent, having already decided to vote for whatever Quentin wanted.

Having heard all the facts, Quentin will tell the others that he agreed with Jax, that the *Evening Show* invitation *is* probably a trap, but he'll accept the offer anyway.

Seventeen days later in New York City, Phibs, Esabell and Jax will watch backstage as Quentin shakes hands with Roger Heffer, a fifty-five-year-old with a pronounced chin and hairpiece, the studio audience cheering throughout. Quentin won't be nervous, but he will be suspicious of Roger's cheeky grin the moment he sits down.

"So, Quentin," Roger will start, "tell us about Unplugged."

Quentin will hesitate, his eyes directly on Roger's. "Unplug."

"What?"

"It's Unpl—"

"Sorry? Come again?"

Quentin will give an annoyed smile. "Unplug. Not past tense."

"You're right. Unplug."

"Present tense. Direct."

Roger will nod broadly. "Like an order. *Unplug ze computers!*" The crowd will laugh immaturely at that.

Quentin will simply stare, suppressing his frustration. "A philosophy."

"Ah!" Roger will flash another phony grin. "So then tell us about your… *philosophy*."

Quentin will look at all those faces in the crowd. A cough somewhere. He'll fidget in his seat. "Over the past forty years, digital dependency in America has grown to a level simply out of control, affecting every aspect of life, every industry. It's the only way we can make friends or date or have sex, you know."

"Speak for yourself," Roger will quip. Lots of applause and laughs at that.

But Quentin won't laugh, awkwardly powering through his spiel. "And at first it was just social media. Algorithms. Twitter abuse. That was fine. But then COVID happened, and suddenly everyone was made aware how much digital a consumer was willing to tolerate. Working from home. Streaming everything. Ordering clothes online. Food online. Booze online. Drugs online. Free porn online. Then inflation happened, twice. Then the Recession. Then all the schools went digital, and then the workplaces again, and sports, church services, and now we're here. Everything's online now to save overhead. In-person education is now a luxury. Eating in a restaurant is now a luxury. Going to a bar or watching live music is now a luxury. And all the blue-collar jobs — package deliveries, truck drivers, waiters, taxis, factory workers, steve-dores — they're all AI now. Why pay a high school dropout minimum wage, a lifetime of benefits and a pension when you can have the economic virtues of slave labor and none of the human rights violations?"

The audience will react uneasily to that one.

"And then the Boomers started dying," Quentin will con-tinue, "their kids getting millions overnight. Next thing you know there's Millennial CEOs, Millennial board members, Millennial non-profits. They could finally start living the way their parents did, but what did they do instead? They hoarded all the wealth, controlled all the information, rigged the rules to keep everything for themselves, and then they passed all that debt and grief onto their kids. That's why you guys need to keep us online. We're the ones giving you the clicks and views that pay for everything, but that's making an entire generation of people, the ones without perfect bodies or technical wizardry, fall through the cracks. It's depriving tens of millions of people from experiencing a full, real life outside of a heavily mathematical, sanitized, overly vetted bubble."

Roger will nod with a hint of awkwardness. "But of course the vast wealth of knowledge the Internet brings—"

"What wealth of knowledge?"

"There are entire subreddits dedicated to philosophy, his-tory. Wikipedia alone... They don't dumb down their in-formation to a mass audience."

"I'm not talking about Wikipedia."

"You've got podcasts on every subject imaginable, executed in unique and creative ways. The entire history of music and film and TV is at our fingertips. You can put a VR headset on and walk through the Grand Canyon. You can watch a live concert or a basketball game or a hockey game from the front row. Your generation has access to so much more than any other generation before it, and you just wanna… dismiss it all as a mistake that should never have happened?"

"That's not life," Quentin will retort. "That's screens. Pictures. Loudness. No camera can properly capture scale. You can't send wind over Wi-Fi. You can't AirDrop smells or touch or sensations or stomach swirlies. I mean, sure, it can get pretty close at times. I'll admit that. But after forty years, we still can't seem to get a hold on how to digitally recreate how great it feels to be alive! To be in the world! Watching a movie isn't the same as going out to a movie theater, sitting in a dark room, feeling your seat vibrate, hearing other people next to you sharing that experience. Or going to a concert, or a football game, a baseball game, basketball, hockey, feeling that energy, that excitement. Real life simply cannot be simulated, no matter how hard we try."

Roger will sit up a bit, placing his elbows on his desk. "I have two kids at home. They're just about to get out of high school. Believe me, they don't wanna go to a movie theater. They don't wanna go to a concert. They don't wanna travel. They don't even want to leave the house. They *want* to stay in and play video games, and hang out with their friends, and scroll the Internet for hours."

"No, they don't!" Quentin will say with a disgusted scowl. "My God, no they don't! They've just been told their whole lives that they have no choice but to settle for what they have! You're right, we do have a wealth of knowledge in our pockets at all times, and being raised with that power has made all of us very smart, incredibly smart, but the Internet is telling us that intelligence doesn't matter, that wisdom doesn't matter. What matters, apparently, is how we look! How many followers we have! How many likes we have! How important it is to be liked! How important it is to get those little numbers to go up! That you have to make a fool of yourself to reach more hypothetical people! That is NOT what the smartest generation in human history should be giving a crap about! Our standards and our priorities have been warped because the only world we have ever known is online! We can't get lost anymore! We can't be spontaneous! We can't be bored! We can't just turn off and relax and be present! We can't be private citizens! That is not natural! That was imposed on us, ever since we were born, and I think it's time we correct that error of bad parenting." Before Roger gets a chance to respond, Quentin will turn away and look directly at Camera 1. "Which is why the Unplug Movement is starting a nationwide boycott of all social media, streaming services, dating apps, hookup apps, Metaverses, online subscriptions, smartphone usage, all web surfing of any kind, anything that generates revenue from advertising and data collection, starting this New Year's Day, January 1st, 2047. Instead, we'll go to grocery stores ourselves. We'll buy our clothes in person. We'll only consume physical media. Live music. We'll go to bookstores and movie theaters. We'll meet people in bars and restaurants and clubs and malls. We'll get our news through the official Unplug Newsletter, released every week by an unbiased team of expert curators, both through email and a postal equivalent. If you are interested in joining our cause, simply send your name, address, email and phone number to our new member outreach headquarters at MIT, or email us directly at enroll@unplug.org.

And be sure to tweet out your support using #Unplug. That is 'Unplug,' U-N-P-L-U-G. Present tense." Quentin will let out a nice sigh, thankful he got all the essentials out.

Roger will draw his brows in a bit. "You do realize having a hashtag *is* using the Internet, right?"

"Of course I do."

"Not to mention an email newsletter will require your members to keep paying for the Internet."

"It's just until newspapers come back the way vinyl did. When enough people switch over and the price of postage goes down, we'll discontinue the email version."

"Yeah, but *philosophically* — that's the word that you used — it's a bit all over the place."

"You can't free people from the Matrix without actually going into the Matrix."

"And that's how you see yourself? Freeing people from the Matrix? You think you're in a movie?"

"No. This is a serious adult issue."

"Oh! If you wanna talk about this like *adults...*" Roger will don a bit of a scowl. "A boycott on that scale would crash the economy overnight. The NASDAQ alone would cease to exist—"

"It's not gonna be overnight. We won't have enough people committed by January 1st—"

"Alright then. You heard it here first."

"But it will work eventually. And the market will have no choice but to react to what its customers are asking for, or else they go out of business."

"So you don't care that millions of Americans will lose their jobs because of you?"

"They'll change their jobs, not lose them." Quentin will shrug. "And hey, I'm sorry, that's life."

The audience will mutter at that, making Quentin nervous.

"'That's life,'" Roger will repeat, inhaling through gritty teeth. "Pretty harsh words from someone concerned about the betterment of humanity."

"Doing the morally right thing *is* better for humanity."

"Oh, so you think stereotyping an entire generation is morally right?"

"Holding that generation accountable for the damage they've done to their children, to the future they won't live long enough to see, yeah, absolutely." Quentin will swallow his dry throat, those bright stage lights making him sweat. "C'mon, our whole lives we were called Children of COVID! Like we're a freaking disease! We're not a disease!"

"Children of the COVID *pandemic*," Roger will calmly correct. "Raised during the pandemic, which is true."

"We're more than the circumstances of our birth."

"Doesn't change the fact that it's true. The Baby Boomers were spawned in the postwar baby boom. The Millennials were raised in the new millennium. 'Child of COVID' is not a slur."

"Considering you guys were the ones that named us that, of course you'd think that. But it is. You know why?" Quentin will pause for effect. "'Child.' That's all we'll be to you, isn't it?"

"Children fetishize dragons and princesses and magic. Things that aren't real. And I think it's funny, you telling me what it was like before the Internet, because you have no idea what you're talking about. To you it's probably just as fantastical as *Harry Potter*."

"The real world? I don't know what the real world is like? Yeah, you're absolutely right. And coming from a Millennial,

the generation famous for fetishizing the 80s for three decades, yeah, I wouldn't say it's unprecedented." Quentin will sit
back, a frumpy frown growing. "'We learned from watching
you.' There. That's an 80s quote, ain't it?"

Roger won't know what to say to that.

"What we're doing..." Quentin will emphasize slowly, "...is
no different from what the Boomers did with their parents.
There's another precedent for you: the Hippies. Remember
them? They literally invented the entire concept of counterculture."

A subtle grin will curl on the ends of Roger's lips. "They
invented a lot of things."

"They saw how broken their society was. They were told
to live with it or else, but they said no, and that changed everything, didn't it?"

"Yes, but—"

"Even today, the very rights and standards we were raised
to believe to be the soul of America were almost entirely invented by the Boomers."

Roger will chuckle at that. "You know, I'm surprised you
admire them so much."

"Why wouldn't I be? They saved the nation. They fought
for civil rights. Racial discrimination. Nuclear disarmament.
Vietnam. Women's rights. Gay rights—"

"I agree."

"And that's surprising to you?"

Roger will stare. "Considering they invented the Internet,
uh... yeah. It does."

Quentin's blood will go cold. He won't even hear the audience's shocked whispers.

Roger will furrow his brow. "You *did* know the Boomers
invented the Internet, right? Tim Berners-Lee, Bill Gates,

Steve Jobs, they're all Boomers. I mean…" He'll laugh. "That's pretty basic info, right? Unless you want to credit us with that too, but, I mean, we were in… what, elementary school, middle school by then?"

Quentin's face will go numb.

"Oh, and all that other stuff you said," Roger will continue, waving his hand, "labor unions, cutting out blue-collar jobs, in-person workplaces, schools, that wasn't us either. We didn't have the House, the Senate, the Presidency, the Supreme Court. We didn't do anything." Roger will throw in a childish scoff. "I mean, it's no wonder you admire the Boomers so much. You're doing exactly what they did. Blaming us for all their…" He'll have to hard-stop himself. "Phooey."

Quentin will swallow, shrinking into his seat like he's ten again.

Roger will tilt his head. "Wasn't that the whole point of your little… midnight, coked-out *Mein Kampf*? How morally wrong it is to punish someone for the sins of their parents?"

No one will talk or even move in the studio for a full five seconds.

"Alright!" Roger will exclaim, grinning wide for the cameras. "Thank you for joining us, Quentin! Quentin Wagner everybody!" The audience will stand and applaud, cheering loudly because the sign said so. Roger will too, gesturing down at Quentin. "Leader of the Unplugged!" He'll throw Quentin a cheeky wink.

Quentin will only scowl back.

After the show, Quentin and Phibs will sit in the back of a two-man driverless Ridr on their way back to their hotel. "God, you shoulda heard Esabell and Jax backstage," Phibs will say with a big grin on his face. "They were screaming at the TV every time Roger opened his mouth."

Quentin won't respond. He'll simply stare out the window at all those shiny Times Square advertisements whizzing by.

"I've never watched anything with other people in the same room before." Phibs will laugh. "If this is what having friends is like, I fucking love it!"

"We really didn't think it through, did we?" Quentin will murmur.

"I actually think you did pretty good job, considering. We knew it was gonna get thorny."

"That's not what I'm talking about."

"What then?" Phibs will look over with dumb innocent eyes. "What?"

But Quentin will simply sigh. "Nothing," he'll whisper. "Forget it."

And Phibs will.

5.

aftermath

Jaymeigh Grady-Smith-Waterhouse-Price will still be up when *The Evening Show* airs later that night, working on her thesis in her Berkeley apartment, tuning out her roommates with Mozart over noise-canceling headphones. They'll still be talking about it when she leaves her room to make herself a sandwich. Normally she ignores whatever they're saying, but upon hearing the word "Unplug," her attention will wander over. That can't be the same Unplug Ghiuliyette told her about months ago, can it?

Jaymeigh will do a Wikipedia deep dive out of curiosity, spilling over to Google to catch those first reactionary tweets and AI-generated articles. Yes, it is in fact the same Unplug, and that TrueSwitch post Ghiuliyette was so passionate about was written by the very guy Roger Heffer had on his show, that Quentin Wagner dude. She kinda wants to watch it now.

And Jaymeigh will, instantly regretting it by the end. What an atrociously lopsided interview. The poor guy just wanted to talk, and all Roger did was shit on every word he said. Maybe Roger didn't take the same Journalistic Integrity 303 Jaymeigh aced last year, or maybe he did and was simply pretending not to know how to give a textbook perfect interview. Jaymeigh will feel disgusted either way, having never felt so badly for another human being as she did for Quentin that night.

Looking at all those tweets will make her brain feel even worse. Thank God she doesn't waste her time with all that. Hundreds of people her parents' age all making the same joke: "Oh he's unplugged alright!" each one thinking they're the first clever bastard to come up with that punchline. And the memes! Jesus, how predictable! None of them particularly insightful, just surface-level associations, like how hypocritical it is that an organization determined to end the Internet couldn't have happened without the Internet in the first place. Oh, and those loner investigators midnight-digging into Unplug's background… God, they're so annoying. A popular revelation going around is how Quentin paid the airfare of one of their members, Jax Halsteder, so he could fly out to California and promote their movement when a simple hashtag would've sufficed. Tweet upon tweet calling that hypocritical, and yet the same morons are calling them hypocrites for having a hashtag in the first place! How stupid they all are! How incendiary!

Jaymeigh will smack her browser shut, thankful to be out of that nest of vipers, determined to move on with her life, but not without contributing one last thought of her own: all those people trying so hard to tear Quentin down are only proving his point.

Three days later, Thanksgiving dinners across the country will still be talking about "Unplugged," Millennial parents mocking Quentin himself, his age, his appearance, his lack of digital footprint. At one such gathering outside Austin, Texas, fifty-one-year-old Cal Vectors will be sipping an IPA at his brother Jim's luxurious suburban home, bored out of his mind. Jim's friends, all of them wealthy content creators, will be rehashing the same Anti-Unplugged talking points for about the umpteenth time.

"They have no idea how easy they have it," Flora Menny will declare, once a beauty guru, now a producer. "They don't even pay for their own Internet!"

The entire gathering will laugh except for Cal.

"And who's *he* to speak for them?" Gabe Hennigan will ask, a trick-shot/parkour YouTuber. "What is he, thirty?"

"Twenty-seven," Cal will mumble.

"Whatever. He's a nobody."

"A nobody we're still talking about." Cal will crack open another IPA, feeling mischievous now. "Probably because he's actually got a point and we're all too afraid to admit it. Some of us, at least."

Gabe will glare at Cal. "Who the fuck asked you?"

"You asked who he is to speak for them. Even if he is on the borderline of Gen Z and Gen A, he's still more entitled to talk about it than we are, wouldn't you say?"

"My kids are Gen A, asshole. How many you got?"

"None."

"Exactly, so shut the fuck up."

Everyone will laugh and *oh-ho-ho!* Cal will grimace from the humiliation.

Jim, Cal's brother, will wander over from the kitchen. "Cal, what are you doing?"

Gabe will stand up to go watch football. "Your brother's a fucking asshole."

"How many tablets you give 'em?" Cal will ask Gabe.

Gabe will stop and look back at Cal. "What?"

"Pads. How many you give 'em?"

"That's none of your fucking business."

Cal will stand, swaying on his feet. "See, if there's nothing wrong with it, why's it such a sensitive issue for you? Is it because you kinda get it?"

Jim will try to slip the bottle out of Cal's hand. "Alright, that's enough for you."

Cal will recoil. "No! I've heard y'all bitch all night. It's time for me to bitch."

"We already know, Cal," Jenn, Gabe's wife, will whine. "You work at a fucking movie theater. A boycott would make you a ton of money. Of course you like it."

"And that's why you hate it. Cause you'd lose a ton of money."

"At least we have money to lose," Gabe will murmur.

Cal will laugh. "Oh-ho-ho! Here we go!"

Jim will try to lure Cal away. "Cal, c'mon."

Cal will whip away from Jim. "No! Fuck off!" He'll take a step toward Gabe. "I did the same thing you did. I quit my job to do what I really wanted, just like the rest of y'all. I didn't care about the money. If I cared about the money, I would've been a lawyer or a doctor or some shit, but no. I wanted to be a fucking movie house guy."

Gabe will scoff. "An usher."

"Parkour douche say what?"

"I get twenty million views a week. How much do you make?"

"Same I did at the start."

"Twenty-five years ago."

"Yeah, well..." Cal will shrug. "I like it. I still like it. I don't have to worry about providing for anyone else. I've got friends there. I make people happy. I get to see *my* viewers." Cal will sip more beer. "And yeah, sure, I'd love more asses in the seats.

Who wouldn't? I'm just saying..." Cal will blink a bunch, trying to remember. "I'm saying... Like him or not, he's got a point. He's got a real, actual point. Maybe we have gone a bit too far with the digital shit. All I'm saying is... he's saying for us to reel it in a bit. Is that too much to fucking ask or something?"

Jim will gently lead Cal away. "C'mon, man."

"No, I'm just..."

"I know, I know. Let him go."

Cal will frown and reluctantly follow his brother outside, closing the sliding door. "Thanks for the turkey, I guess."

"What's wrong with you?" Jim will ask. "I had to beg Beth to invite you this year. Why do you have to be such an asshole?"

"Come on!" Cal will hock his throat and spit on the grass. "You know how much shit they made me eat over the years."

"And I call them out every—"

"No, you don't." Cal will frown at his brother. "I was just playing it safe, Jim. I didn't ask to go down with a ship. I just didn't want to spend thousands on a gamble. But now their thousands turned into millions and they think that makes them fucking gods or something." Cal will pull out a pack of cigarettes. "Want one?"

Jim will smile a bit. "Sure."

Cal will light up two and hand one over. "Now the tables have turned. I'm going up and *they're* going down. Can't blame me for wanting to enjoy it a little."

Jim will blow out some smoke, checking the kitchen window for signs of the ol' ball and chain. "Why do you hate them so much?"

Cal will flick ash onto Jim's sod. "God, if you had any idea what it's like to go to work every day at that place."

"I can imagine."

"No, *again*, you can't," Cal will say curtly. "That's the fucking point. Every day I'm in there with those old people... And they're just so happy to be there. To share an experience like that. To talk film with other film lovers. And I *work there!* They know my name. They ask me how I am. And Mr. G fucking loves me. He trusts me. He lets me plan the programs and read off trivia on the weekends. And every so often I see a kid in there, and I just wanna cry. It makes me so happy thinking about that little kid passing it along to their kids, and I think people one day will figure out what's going on there is STILL going on, it's STILL just as amazing as it always was. But then I go home and talk to literally anyone at Casper's, or the Diner, or the bus, and all anyone has to say about it is how expensive it is or how stupid and dirty it is or that there isn't a difference between that and watching something on their phone, *and this is from people who haven't been in a movie theater for twenty-five years!* If they'd been there once and had a problem with it, I'd understand, but so many people THINK THEY KNOW, but they don't! They don't, and I do, because I'M the one who's there every morning! You have no idea how infuriating it is to literally tell someone how it is and for them to tell you it's not! And they do it about EVERYTHING! Fucking everything! They're doing it to this kid right now! This Quentin guy! They should be giving him a fucking Nobel Peace Prize for what he's doing, but no one our age wants to admit that maybe, just maybe, he's actually one thousand percent right about this! And that PISSES... ME... the FUCK... OFF!"

Jim will blow out smoke, snuffing his cigarette early. "I'll come by next week, alright?"

"You keep saying that. I don't believe you anymore."

"Well, I'll try this time. Alright? Really."

Cal will smirk. "Hey, no rush." He'll puff out smoke. "In a couple months, it might just be your only option."

Just as the 24-hour news cycle finally moves on from that *Evening Show* interview, *Saturday Night Live* will revive the discourse with its "Unplugged" cold open. Lots of jokes revolving around Quentin's physical appearance, particularly his naturally unkempt hair (featuring punchlines like "The roots go to my brain!" and Quentin having never heard of a haircut cause he's not on the Internet). A running gag of Quentin getting triggered every time Roger makes an accidental Internet pun (RAM, memory, network, web, mouse, address, so on). A particularly "hysterical" moment when Quentin quotes an actual statistic from memory, prompting Roger to admit that Quentin actually said something intelligent, to which Quentin will quip, "Thanks, I saw it on YouTube." An entire tangent involving Roger questioning Jax's LA plane ticket, a conversation that never actually happened in the real interview. And just as Quentin reveals his perfect world (everyone sitting around in chairs, staring silently into space), it'll be revealed that "Quentin" is actually a malfunctioning robot, prompting Roger to look at the camera and give that famous *SNL* catchphrase.

The *SNL* cold open will go viral on YouTube in the hours afterward, drawing the attention of millions of people who never would've heard of Unplug without it. Among those first introduced to "Unplugged" that night will be Representative Douglas Cameron (D-CA). Sixty years old. Bald. Crotchety. Cameron, after watching the original *Evening Show* interview to get the *SNL* jokes, will be so angry by it that he'll impulsively drunk-tweet toxic vitriol late into the night, specifically how stupid and spoiled all Children of COVID have become if they believe such asinine bullshit.

The next morning, November 25, 2046, Cameron's staff will reprimand the Representative for his very public "man yells at clouds" midnight meltdown and book a last-minute damage control interview on CNN for him to set the record straight.

"You're one of the Unplugged Movement's most vocal dissenters," host Kathy Blower will read off the teleprompter with automated ease, her mind somewhere else, too preoccupied with the latest drug-fueled antics of her cheating whore of a wife. "What is it about Quentin Wagner, you think, that attracts so many Children of COVID?"

"I want to clarify something," Cameron will reply, reciting his rehearsed speech with automated ease, his mind somewhere else, too preoccupied with the latest drug-fueled antics of his piece of shit son. "Unplugged as a movement I absolutely abhor. It's a microcosm of the immaturity of Gen A, a purely emotional reaction devoid of logic or common sense, and it makes me sick thinking about so many spoiled rotten children downright encouraging a systematic plunge into a literal Dark Ages. But contrary to what many might think out there, I don't have any problem with Quentin Wagner as an individual."

Kathy will snap back to the present. "You don't?" she'll ask, out of character.

"I've seen the interview. I think he's very intelligent for his age. Resourceful. Great under pressure. Well-educated. Self-aware. It's no wonder he developed such a following. He has fantastic leadership skills. However, at the same time, that's what makes him all the more dangerous. The same qualities that make him stand out are the very qualities of a gaslighter.

He's a masterful manipulator that found himself a flock willing to eat up his nonsense. And he knows it's nonsense. Any smart person would think so."

"You're giving him *way* too much credit. That Manifesto—"

"The Manifesto was written under duress. Any perceived incoherence is simply a side effect that comes about with emotional venting… and no wonder, considering he wrote it only a day after he tried to kill himself."

Quentin, watching the interview alone in his Emerson College headquarters, will feel his blood turn cold.

"Is that confirmed?" Kathy will ask Cameron.

"My team did some digging," Cameron will respond. "Six hours before he posted on TrueSwitch, Quentin checked himself into the emergency room with facial bleeding and broken fingers. Hospital records show he admitted to attempting suicide the night before, hurting himself on the bathroom mirror. Now, does that sound like a person with all his marbles intact? Hard to say. But it certainly explains the rambling incoherence of his post. And yet, despite that, it still bears conventional spelling and grammar as well as a persuasive overall structure. He has a Bachelor's in Creative Writing from Emerson College. This guy is a writer at his core. I wrote a memoir myself a few years back. It's not easy. I still get bile thinking back on those early drafts. Good writer, bad writer, doesn't matter. A real writer knows when they wrote garbage, and Quentin Wagner is a real writer that might've gone a bit too far writing a hunk of garbage. But guess what! It went viral! So he doubled down. Who wouldn't? He just tried to kill himself. He had nothing to lose. But now he's got a horde of impressionable young minds he can capitalize off of. He can tell them anything he wants and they'll believe him. So no, I don't have a problem with Quentin Wagner as a person. I *do* have a problem with him lying to his constituents, pretending to believe his own manure, peddling a bogus philosophy. The Unplugged Movement will cost the American taxpayer millions of dollars. Millions of jobs will be lost. And millions of desperate newly-unemployed workers, shocked by the sudden fragility of their own job security, will be thrust into that same suicidal situation Quentin was in! Maybe they won't be as smart as he was. Maybe they won't live to see another day. That blood will be on his hands. I'm telling you, Kathy, if he's as smart as I think—"

Quentin will shut off the TV, disturbed in his marrow, in the deepest crevices of himself. Phibs will be back any second, telling him it's all set up in the Common, that stage he had requested, all the lights and cameras, the crowd of Unpluggers all gathered and ready to go, having no idea that Quentin planned to give the perfect concession speech. The Manifesto was a mistake. He was closing the curtain. Admitting his guilt. Telling everyone to go home.

But not now. Not after this. How dare Cameron stoop that low. How dare he invade his privacy like that, his *offline* privacy. Digging into his darkest days just to discredit him. Dredging up the single most sensitive, tender, private moment of his life, when he felt most alone, when he *thought* he was alone, only for that bastard to blast it out to the world.

How.

Fucking.

Dare.

He.

That night was supposed to be just his. That's what started the whole thing, the fact that he could actually have something that was just his, just something in this fucking world that's off-*fucking*-limits for once, and now it's not. Now it's everyone's. And they're all gonna fucking leave him now because of it.

Phibs will let himself into Quentin's office moments later, curious to hear what Quentin's mysterious announcement's gonna be, like everyone else, only to find Quentin rummaging around his desk drawers. "What's wrong?" Phibs will ask.

Quentin will slam the drawer shut. "I can't find the hole-puncher."

Phibs will wander over. "Why do you need a hole-puncher?"

"Just help me, alright? The metal one with hydraulics. I know it's around here somewhere."

"You're going on in five minutes."

"I know. I'm taking it with me."

"On stage?"

"Yeah."

Jax will walk in. "Cameras all set."

"No cameras." Quentin will whip open a side drawer. "There it is!" He'll lift a shiny steel hole-puncher, holding it up to the light to inspect the length of the gap. "Phibs, get me some rubbing alcohol."

Jax will watch with concern as Phibs hands Quentin a bottle of rubbing alcohol. "No cameras?" he'll ask.

"No cameras," Quentin will repeat, practically shaking as he pours a little alcohol onto the hole-puncher's tooth.

"Why no cameras?"

"People lived a thousand FUCKING years without FUCKING cameras! They don't need 'em to remember a FUCKING speech!"

Jax will get an uneasy feeling in his gut. "What are you gonna say?"

"What do you think I'm gonna say?!" Quentin will click the hole-punch a few times, the hydraulic making a loud popping noise. "We're doubling down, motherfuckers! Tut tut!" He'll kick the office door open. March out. "Someone get me a whiskey!"

The two thousand official members of the Unplug Movement will wait in earnest in front of the makeshift stage in Boston Common. "You okay?" Jax will ask Quentin as they walk across Boylston Street. "You were never nervous before."

"Shut up," Quentin will rasp, downing the double shot of whiskey in his hand, handing the glass back to Phibs. He'll make a queer squealing noise as he swallows.

Phibs will wait with Quentin backstage as Esabell and Jax hurry to shut off all the cameras one-by-one. "I heard what he said," Phibs will whisper discreetly.

Quentin will avoid eye contact with Phibs. "What who said?"

"Cameron." Phibs will hesitate. "Is it true? What he said?"

Quentin will slip into a genuine morose frown. "Which part?"

But Phibs won't say anything more.

Quentin will smirk a bit to himself. He'll shake it off and step up to the curtain.

"Break a leg," Phibs will tell him.

"Get the First Aid Kit," Quentin will mutter, strolling onto the stage with the hole-puncher conspicuously clutched in his right hand.

The crowd will cheer at first, slipping into a confused murmur at the sight of the hole-puncher.

Quentin will stop at center stage, all those lights blinding his eyes, and stare off into space. He'll feel his blood pressure spike in real time. "Thank you, but let me speak."

The crowd will hush down, looking up at Quentin.

Quentin will laugh a bit too hard, his face dripping with sweat. "I can't believe I'm actually doing this... Um..." He'll clear his throat, all numb from the whiskey. "I'm sure the past few days haven't been the easiest for everyone." He'll hesitate, his right hand shaking. "For me especially. I've been the target of a pretty bad media lambasting, particularly from Douglas Cameron last night. I'm sure you've heard. Even just a moment ago, he... He called me names. A liar, actually, and... And the way he talked about... What he says I did the night before... It's simply not true."

Esabell, standing off-stage, will instantly tune out the speech at the sight of the Chekhov's Gun in Quentin's right hand. "What's with the hole-puncher?" she'll ask Jax.

"I don't know," Jax will answer. They'll both look at Phibs standing next to them with a First Aid Kit clutched to his chest. "What are you doing?" Jax will ask him.

"He asked for a First Aid Kit," Phibs will say.

"Why?"

Esabell will get a funny feeling in her stomach. "You can't... kill yourself with a hole-puncher, can you?"

Phibs will take a deep breath. "Guess we're about to find out."

"No way," Jax will say, shaking his head. "He's joking. Has to be."

"...my Manifesto," Quentin will continue, his anger barely stifled. "Calling it garbage and nonsense." He'll pause. "But worse than that, he had the gall to accuse me of faking my own allegiance to this movement. Of me not... *believing* my own Manifesto anymore. That I'm secretly hiding it from you." He'll shake his head some more, fighting through the lie. "No. I know what I said. I meant it. I told you all I was going to boycott the Internet, and I meant it. I told you how committed I was to fighting the greedy corporations for stealing our data, selling it to the highest bidder, using every ounce of their technological power to turn us all into ravenous content junkies! Eliminating free journalism! Personalizing search results and monetizing them! Forcing us to net zero in suffocating cocoons! *And I meant it!*"

The crowd will roar with applause.

"But just in case there's any doubters out there," Quentin will continue, "whether it's you, or you, or Douglas fucking Cameron, here's another one for you." He'll hold up the hydraulic hole-puncher. "I'm gonna hole-punch my earlobe."

"He's not joking," Jax will murmur.

Without a second to spare, Quentin will slip his right earlobe under the anvil and squeeze the hydraulic lever. The puncher will SNAP, the lobe fat instantly breaking with a crooked CRUNCH, and the crowd will GASP and YELL and HOLLER, but louder than any of them will be Quentin screaming "FUUUUCCKK!" as he drops to all fours, the blood-covered puncher bouncing away, warm blood trickling down his neck and onto the stage. Through searing pain, he'll sense Phibs crouched next to him with a First Aid Kit cracked open, already unrolling mounds of gauze with the precise control of a NASCAR pit crew.

Jax will stay where he was, frozen on the wings, mouth agape, emboldened by such a display of sheer badassery, jealous of not being the one to commit such a powerful act.

Esabell, similarly stone-faced, will be more focused on the crowd, realizing the importance of such a dramatic event not being filmed, just people experiencing a moment — a fucked up, unpredictable moment — hundreds of real eyeballs and memory banks working at full force. How magical that is. How powerful. All hail Quentin!

And Quentin will struggle to his feet, two fingers squeezing bloody gauze onto his gaping earlobe, and he'll channel all that pain toward the shocked and disoriented faces before him: "I fucking said it, didn't I?! And I fucking *did it*, didn't I?! Don't you fucking forget it! Don't you listen to any bullshit trying to paint me off as some charlatan or a nobody! I AM FOR REAL! They know this and they're scared shitless! That's why they're still talking about us! They're digging for anything, ANYTHING, to discredit us! Because if we're really just a bunch of silly kids with a stupid plan, they wouldn't even give us the time of day! No! The truth is, they're scared of us! They're scared because they see what we know, what we can do, how far we're willing to go, and they know we'll succeed! That it's gonna work! That they're FUCKED!" Quentin will stop to catch his breath.

The crowd will be silent, too rapt to cheer.

"I know it's hard," Quentin will rasp, "listening to everyone telling us how wrong we are. Calling us misguided and stupid and spoiled and lazy and... and *crazy!* And I know some of you, myself included, might feel that maybe they're right, maybe we are getting a little too carried away with ourselves. But I want you to do something for me. The next time that happens... the next time... this is what you do. When your parents or your teachers or your professors or your coworkers or your boss or some newsman or some washed-up Millennial politician like Douglas Cameron tells you you're wrong, or scolds you for being here, doing this, daring to unplug, when they call you names or try to realign you, go onto their Facebooks. Go onto their Twitters, their TikToks, their Reddits, their Instagrams, their Tumblr feeds, their YouTube channels, and go back years, decades, to when they were your age right now. Look at them and watch. Watch them stupidly swallow cinnamon, and throw themselves in front of cars, and accidentally set themselves on fire. Watch them play dirty party games, making jokes about eating pussy and bestiality. Watch them twerk and griddy and floss and dougie and crank dat and pop their pussies to childish bullshit. And don't just watch. Remember. Remember all of it. Because when those people, those 'grown-ups,' tell you you need to respect them, to fear them, to listen to them, remember THAT was what they were doing when they were your age! AND WHAT ARE *YOU* DOING?! ARE YOU DANCING?! ARE YOU LAUGHING?! NO! YOU'RE CHANGING THE *FUCKING* WORLD!"

And the loudest of roars will cry out in the night, from Long Wharf to Fenway, from Mike's Pastry to Chinatown, all along the Green Line, the Red Line, even the Orange Line, to every brownstone and Dunkin' in between.

6.

boycott

The Unplug Boycott will begin as planned on January 1, 2047. Several thousand Internet junkies will suddenly stop clicking overnight, stop scrolling, stop posting, stop liking, stop disliking, so on. It won't add up to much more than a blip on the data of the ISPs, and said data will be used by the media to roast Unplug, labeling the Boycott "an embarrassing failure" on January 2. But that blip won't undo itself. It'll grow slowly but surely over the next six weeks, culminating in an unending wave that ultimately washes away the Internet dependent economy and plunges the world into a golden age (or Dark Age, depending on who you ask) of human existence.

Decades later, when future historians try to understand the day-to-day timeline of the famous Unplug Movement, they won't be able to understand what made the Boycott so darn successful in its infant stages, their world being one of distant, emotionless objectivity. Even Unplug's high command at the time won't be able to understand why it's working so well, nor will their enemies in the media or the billions of bystanders watching from the outside, eager to see who wins. They simply won't get it because of their limited human perspective, clouded by an incessant need to assign logic to everything, anything to give a big complex issue a one-and-done explanation.

The only ones who'll know just why Unplug worked so well will be the early boycotters themselves. Ironically, the secret to the Boycott's success will be the very thing that plugged the world in the first place, the most valuable currency in the digital world, the secret sauce of all capitalism, the very thing advertisers pour billions of dollars to try and simulate, the very thing no one seems to be able to do on purpose despite so many achieving by accident: the physical sensation the Boycott had on the human body.

Ghiuliyette Wintergrass, one of the earliest boycotters, will instantly notice a change on the morning of January 1. A strange hole in her world. A routine of sorts that simply didn't exist anymore. A few days later, she'll notice how better her sleep has been. Like actual sleep. And after a week, she'll notice how well she's been retaining thoughts and memories. The world will seem so big around her, and yet her life will feel so much more manageable. There'll be significantly less pressure for her to be aware of everything everywhere all at once. To be more. To be better. Not just perpetually, exponentially. Quickly too, so quickly, before it's all too late. Whatever that means. And silence will seem noticeably quieter to Ghiuliyette. She always thought she had anxiety and depression despite no official diagnosis, but they'll be gone too. She'll find herself calmer, more optimistic. And all this she'll figure out on her own, not because of a potentially manipulative third party. Her Internet addiction generated that shit, she'll realize. She had been holding herself back, flocking to communities that only validated her fears instead of challenging them. Those forums and subreddits, accounts and feeds, those places she once saw as desirable havens, filled with same-suffering allies, will suddenly look like heroin dens in retrospect. And she'll find herself enjoying the little things. Sunshine coming in through a window. Walking out in the woods. Trees diffusing the light. Going out on walks will raise Ghiuliyette's confidence. She'll go out to the park and smile at the sight of other Unpluggers smiling back at her, an unspoken understanding between them. And she'll make friends, real friends this time, in real social spaces no less. Libraries. Shopping malls. Record stores. Whatever news she does get, thanks to her weekly Unplug Newsletter in her mailbox every Monday, will seem so interesting and intriguing to her, all that time-wasting chaff thrown aside for only the things worth knowing about. And she'll tell everyone how great it feels to unplug. A lot of them will be skeptical of her enthusiasm, but even if nine out of ten of them vehemently refuse to try it, the one that does will suddenly *get it*, and the word will spread on. And it'll feel so self-inspired, even though Quentin already predicted it in his TrueSwitch Manifesto. It will be that misinterpretation of self-generation, that lucky trick played on the human brain — the greatest data source of them all — that will make the Boycott stick in those early days.

Jaymeigh will be proof-reading her thesis, a thorough biographical profile of Representative Natasha Mnozhynskyi, "Ms. M," her idol, in UC Berkeley's Doe Memorial Library, when her phone will blast its ringtone out of nowhere. Jaymeigh will quickly silence it, surprised to see Ghiuliyette's name on the caller ID. A phone call. An actual phone call. Jaymeigh will tentatively answer it, worried to death. "Hello?"

"Jaymeigh, it's Ghiuliyette."

"I know. What's wrong? What happened?"

"Nothing's wrong."

Jaymeigh will blink. "You're just… calling me?"

"Well, I do have a question. That guy you read a lot… Dostoevsky?"

Jaymeigh will hesitate. "Yeah?"

"Like, I'm at the bookstore right now, and they've got a lot by him here. I was just wondering, since you're the expert and all, what you recommend."

Jaymeigh will hesitate again, feeling her face go numb. "By Dostoevsky?"

"Yeah, you know, for someone who's never read him."

"You wanna read Dostoevsky?"

"Yeah. I have all this free time now that I unplugged, so I thought, 'Why not try it out?' Oh, I actually recognize this one!"

"Which one?"

"*The Brothers Kazamov.*"

"*Karamazov.*"

"Yeah, that one. That's his big one, right? It must be for a reason."

"Honestly, if you're really serious about 19th Century Russian Literature, you really should start with Tolstoy."

"I don't see that one here."

"No, Leo Tolstoy, another author. Much more accessible to first timers. Start with *Anna Karenina*."

"I thought you said to start with that Leo guy."

"That's the title. *Anna Karenina* by Leo Tolstoy."

"*Anna Karenina.* Got it."

"Oh, and make sure you get the right English translation. The most popular ones are from the early 1900s and they're all dry as dirt."

"Oh… uh…"

"Just go to customer service and ask for the Peavear and Volokhonsky translation of *Anna Karenina*."

A pause over the phone.

Jaymeigh will roll her eyes. "*The Oprah one*," she'll groan. "Ask for the Oprah one. They'll know what you mean."

"Oprah. *Anna*. Tolstoy. Okay! Great! Thanks!"

"Just try it out, and if you like it, then we'll talk about breaking you into Dostoevsky."

"Great! God, this is so much fun! Thanks a ton!" Ghiuli-yette will hang up fast.

Jaymeigh will let her phone arm fall to her side, a frozen cringe on her face. What the fuck is going on?

One month into the Boycott, Cal Vectors will clock into the Prudential Movie House in downtown Austin, just like he had every day for the past twenty-five years, only to find the place noticeably busier inside. Lots of young people. College aged. Some high schoolers too. Weirdly enough, they're all wearing the same jackets, big denim ones with sewn-on logos (Blu-Rays, records, canoe paddling, hiking, acoustic guitars), like the Boy Scout patches he had growing up. Curiouser to Cal will be the other shared accessory among the newcomers: gauged ears.

The Prudential Movie House will be even busier the next day, and the next, and the next, until it's a full house by Friday. Cal and his boss, the lovable Mr. G, will be beside themselves. They've made more in one week than they had in entire years, finally having enough to refurbish the second theater. The repairs to Auditorium 2 will finish two weeks later, and they'll find themselves with *double* full houses every Saturday night.

Intrigued by the sudden revival, Cal will gather the courage one day to sit behind three young men in the back row, adorned with patches on denim and gauges in their ears like all the others. He'll lean over and whisper over the afternoon coming attractions, "Excuse me, fellas."

The three young men will flinch, whipping their heads around. Their first instinct will be unease at the sight of the Millennial sitting behind them. But he obviously works at the badass Prudential Movie House, the one all their friends told them about, so he's probably one of the good ones. "Yeah?" the first one will ask, a twenty-year-old named Eean.

"You guys are doing the Unplugged thing, aren't you?"

"*Unplug*," the second one will correct, a nineteen-year-old named Gozer.

"Yes." Cal will nod apologetically. "'Unplug.' My mistake."

Gozer will cautiously nod back, acknowledging Cal's sincerity. "It's alright. You didn't know."

"I didn't mean to bother you guys. I've just been seeing a lot of you kids around lately and I wanted to know why you're all wearing denim jackets with patches on 'em."

"It's a 60s thing," the third young man will say, Gozer's sixteen-year-old brother Zuul. "The Hippies wore them."

"It's in their honor," Gozer will add. "They're our heroes. Trailblazers of counterculture itself."

Cal will jut his chin at Eean's ears. "What about the gauges? Isn't that more of a 90s thing?"

"That's for Quentin," Eean will answer.

"Quentin Wagner?"

"When Douglas Cameron tweeted all that shit about him and lied about him on CNN, Quentin got so pissed that he got a whole crowd of people in front of a stage and hole-punched his earlobe."

Cal will stare. "He hole-punched his ear in front of you guys?"

"Oh no, we weren't there," Zuul will say. "I really *really* wanted to go, but Mom wouldn't let me go out on a school night. Until I unplugged, that is."

"Jesus, Zuul, you're not supposed to say that word!" Gozer will hiss at him.

"It's the past tense! What am I supposed to say?!"

"Some of our friends were there," Eean will say to Cal. "Apparently it was really badass."

"Wait a minute..." Zuul will say, turning to Eean. "Quentin didn't do it because of Cameron. He was just doing it for fun. That's what Fil Bailey said."

"No, it was because of what Cameron said."

"You're both wrong," Gozer will say. "Quentin didn't do it on any stage. It happened during one of their biweekly meetings in that church basement. Only Jax, Esabell and Phibs saw him do it."

"Uh-uh!" Eean will snipe. "Kryss Crown told me Don-a Kohl told Gym Carr and Roggre Carpin that it happened in Boston Common in broad daylight in front of a million people out of protest because of what Cameon said."

"It wasn't in reaction to anything, I tell you!" Zuul will counter. "It was just a spontaneous piece of performance art." He'll look at Cal with a smile. "He didn't even feel it, apparently."

"Since WHEN?!" Gozer will shout, prompting some audience members to shush at them.

"That's what Theresa Haberdashery said."

"She wasn't there!" Eean will interject.

"Her sister was! She told her he didn't feel a thing... and yet he felt EVERYTHING."

"They're all liars!" Gozer will declare. "NONE OF THEM were there! It was in the church basement, I tell you!"

"Shut the fuck up!" Zuul will say with a laugh. "Rycchaard Patel was in the front row and got blood sprayed all over him, remember?"

Cal will smile, very entertained. "What about you guys? Did it hurt for you?"

All three men will furrow their brows. "What?" Gozer will ask.

"When you hole-punched yourselves, did you reach enlightenment?"

"Oh no, no one does it themselves," Eean will answer. "God, we're not fucking psychos. We got ours done at the mall like everyone else."

"It's so fucking cool!" Gozer will geek. "It's a way for us to find each other, you know? Out in the wild!"

"You know what it reminds me of?" Zuul will say. "Remember back to when we were plugged and we'd get a notification on Instagram? It feels a lot like—"

"Shhh!" Eean will hiss as the lights go down. Gozer and Zuul will excitedly face the screen, their mouths agape in wonder at the sight before them, a real movie starting before their eyes.

Cal will leave them be, beaming with pride at the backs of those boys' heads, unexpectedly moved by their passion and reverence for life. He might even be the happiest he's been his whole life. He can't tell. It's been that long.

Billboard will announce late February that it had reintegrated vinyl single sales back into their official criteria. Overnight, "Aquarius/Let the Sunshine In" by the 5th Dimension will inexplicably return to the top of the Hot 100, seventy-eight years since it was last number 1, breaking a new all-time record.

The Conservatives will turn on the Unplug Movement first. (Of course they'll keep calling it "Unplugged" since that's the one they heard first.) After several weeks of watching their sons and daughters gauge their ears, wear goddamn *hippie* clothes, and whine about the many ways this great mother-fucking country did them wrong, the Florida activist organization Moms for Justice will make "The Dangers of Un-plugging" their main talking point of March 2047.

Officer Mike Fitzer of the Sarasota Police Department will be invited to speak at a local chapter of Moms for Justice. He'll walk into that conference room, full to the brim with worried trad wives, assuring himself that he'll be doing good work to-day by putting all their minds at ease.

After an introductory prayer, Officer Fitzer will begin the presentation. He'll click his clicker and reveal slide 1 of his PowerPoint, the Senior yearbook photo of a beautiful eighteen-year-old girl with silky brown hair.

"This was Lynndzee Maeae Brown," Officer Fitzer will start, noting the reaction to his deliberate use of past tense. "Homecoming queen. Prom queen. Head cheerleader. Straight-A student. Valedictorian. Multiple acceptances to the best schools in the country. Just a few months ago, Lynndzee Maeae found out about Unplugged and decided it looked like fun. Everyone else was doing it. Why shouldn't she?" Officer Fitzer will click to the next slide, focusing more on the Moms' revolted reactions than the graphic photo on screen. "This was Lynndzee Maeae two weeks ago. In just a month and a half, she had dropped out of school, moved in with some friends, partied every night, fell into a nasty drug habit, had promis-cuous sex with strangers — often in public places — and mutilated her pretty little lobes with a pair of ugly steel gauges." Officer Fitzer will mercifully click away, leaving only a picture of her smashed-up automobile. "And just last week, she attempted to drive a 60s-style Volkswagen without a built-in autopilot. In doing so, she lost control of the vehicle and collided head-first with a Honda Civic containing a family of four playing Parcheesi."

Jessica Lyn will start sobbing. "Not *Parcheesi!*"

"Yes. Not only did Lynndzee Maeae lose her own life, she also put three innocent people in the hospital." Officer Fitzer will click the screen to black. "Think about how happy she would have been, what good she could have done in this world, if she only stayed on her phone."

The Moms will shake their heads in disappointment, some blessing themselves with the Sign of the Cross.

Officer Fitzer will then un-black the screen, revealing a candid selfie of burly forty-year-old biker with a shaggy beard and gaping ear gauges. "This is Carlton Smith. He took this photo just after he got his ears gauged at the mall. Just a few days later, Carlton was checked into the hospital for a 103° fever due to twin bacterial infections in his earlobes."

More mournful gasps from the Moms, hands on hearts.

Officer Fitzer will nod. "He almost died. Thankfully he pulled through." The Moms will applaud at that. "Worth noting — he really asked me to emphasize this — Carlton is *not* an Unplugger. He's just a buddy of mine who works part-time at the hazardous waste management facility. It is possible that that's how he got his lobes infected, but we'll never know for sure."

"It's just horrible!" Gerri Cunderson will lament. "My Siouxsie has been begging me to let her get her ears gauged. I keep telling her she can die from it, but she won't listen!"

Officer Fitzer will hesitate. "To be honest, I don't think anyone actually dies from gauging. It's a very safe procedure."

"Yes, but she won't be able to get a job because of it."

Officer Fitzer will hesitate again. "No, pretty much all anti-discrimination policies cover piercings."

"But it's still a permanent mutilation!" Kathy Noon will whine, near tears. "And for WHAT?!"

"See, that's what I thought too, but Carlton actually said if you take out the gauge, the hole closes itself up pretty fast."

Kathy will sniff, wiping her nose with a tissue. "Even still."

"Let's get back to the subject at hand." Officer Fitzer will click to the next slide, revealing a timeline chart. "The biggest danger of unplugging is what we call 'digital withdrawal.' It usually develops in the first few days, getting worse by week one until it hits its peak by week three, after which point they tend to be past the point of no return." Officer Fitzer will click to the next slide, a list of bullet-points, pausing a moment so the Moms can catch up with their notes. "The earliest symptom of digital withdrawal is a better memory. I know that sounds like a good thing, but it's in fact very dangerous. A kid going through digital withdrawal puts themself at risk of memory overload. Too much information for them to try and keep track of could overwhelm them, which will lead to increased stress and anxiety. Better memory would also make it harder for your kid to forget traumatic or negative experiences, which can stagnant maturity. They'll have difficulty filtering out irrelevant information, unimportant details. They'll become easily distracted with nonsense, making it harder for them to focus on what's really important. They'll find themselves dwelling on the past too much, particularly past mistakes, which might create feelings of regret or guilt. Better memory also generates pressure for them to always remember everything they hear, which can lead to performance anxiety, fear of failure and impostor syndrome."

Sally Macadoo will raise her hand.

"Please save all your questions for the end." Officer Fitzer will click to the next slide, more bullet points. "The second symptom of digital withdrawal is an excess of sleep. Smartphones emanate blue light, which tricks the eye into thinking it's still daylight, which keeps kids' brains active and alert at all times. Without that blue light, your kid will find themselves getting tired much earlier than normal. Studies have shown Unpluggers tend to sleep eight or nine hours *every night*. Think of all that wasted potential, all the content they could've clicked on instead." Officer Fitzer will move on to the next slide. "The third symptom of digital withdrawal is a surge in foolhardy ambition. Unpluggers like to wander off, often without warning or a backup plan, due to increased levels of curiosity… and we all know what curiosity did to the cat."

The Moms will all nod in unison.

"It killed it," Sally Macadoo will murmur.

"Yes. Because they're more curious, they're more likely to take risks, try out new hobbies, *expensive* hobbies, often involving physical exertion or dangerous movements, like rock climbing or football. By forcing themselves out of their comfort zone, they're more likely to put themselves in a scenario where they have no instinctual groundwork. If something were to go wrong or get dangerous for them, they won't know how to get themselves out of it." Officer Fitzer will click to the next slide. "The fourth and final symptom is an over-abundance of confidence. One of the great things about social media is its ability to keep horny teenagers abstinent, all those pictures of hot girls and buff guys making them too self-conscious to take on risks in the sexual realm. But after they unplug, they'll find themselves free of that social shame. By not obsessing over every little thing wrong with their bodies, there won't be anything stopping them from walking up to a person and having premarital sex with them, which — as we all know — causes unwanted pregnancy and deadly disease."

"Horrible," Janice Gobberfield will whisper as she rapid-jots her notes.

"Long term digital withdrawal can lead to a whole new slew of issues," Officer Fitzer will say, clicking to the next slide. "Without their phones' lifesaving geotracking, they can quite literally be found dead in a ditch somewhere. Similarly, without the safeguard of parental restrictions, they'll be able to see everything there is without an age-appropriate filter, especially the parts of life you'd rather they not see. And without the niche content they formed their whole identity around, they'll find it difficult to adjust to new, unfamiliar things, oftentimes changing themselves in order to fit in. Unpluggers also tend to bear resentment toward their own childhoods, how they were raised, which can be known to split families. And of course, the worst-case scenario: Unpluggers are fifty times more likely to abandon their family and seek independence elsewhere."

The Moms will mournfully sigh at that, multiple hands on multiple hearts.

Officer Fitzer will blacken the screen again. "As dire as this all sounds, there is a way to prevent digital withdrawal from taking control of your child. The newly unplugged are at their most impressionable between days eight and twenty, and the best way to prevent them from going off the deep end is to ease them back onto their phones within that window. If that sounds scary or difficult, I assure you it isn't. I've seen it

happen many times. There is hope. But you have to be tricky
about it. First, as much as you'd want to, do not be firm. That
tends to backfire, further accelerating the digital withdrawal.
Instead, use their interest in analog living against them. You're
not against the Boycott, you're encouraging them to partici-
pate further. They'll let you in. And while you're in, ask them
if they want to go out for a jog or be physically active out of
the house. When they say yes, take them to a gym. All those
TVs and screens in their faces will remind them of how it used
to be. That just might be enough to incite doubt in their new
lifestyle, which they will naturally think is their idea. Another
example: say they want to go on vacation to Yosemite or Yel-
lowstone. Take them to Times Square instead. More screens.
Claustrophobic. Dirty. Smelly. Or if they want to go out to enjoy the nice weather, drag them outside when it's raining or
cloudy. Make them think good weather is actually rare phe-
nomenon. Flame their disappointment. Destroy its allure.
And if an extra push is necessary, drive them at night to a dangerous part of town and leave them there without a phone.
That'll really scare them straight."

"The Dangers of Unplugging" will spread like wildfire
through the Conservative Mom demographic, with mixed results regarding its effectiveness on their kids.

As much as the Democrats really *really* want to be in favor
of Unplug because of how much the Republicans seem to hate
it, they too will turn on the Boycott for reasons of their own.
Unlike the dastardly-expensive-in-person-private-school-ed-
ucated children of the Conservatives, the Liberals' kids will be
predominantly enrolled in the public school system, which by
2047 will be entirely virtual to save the taxpaying voter dollars.
To the Democrats, unplugging isn't just a way for their kids to
passionately put themselves in harm's way; it's literally them

dropping out of school. (Of course the consensus from high-school-aged Unpluggers will be requests for in-person alternatives to public school so they could continue their education without infringing on their new lifestyle, but they're uneducated minors, what do they know? Who do they think's gonna have to PAY for all that?)

And so, in response to the loud, bipartisan backlash against the Unplug Movement, the U.S. Department of Education will create the Dangers of the Unplug Movement Program ("D.U.M.P."), a nationwide series of virtual class visits and school-wide Zoom assemblies designed to debunk students' rose-colored perceptions of unplugging. But there'll be a small oversight to that logic: most students will have no perception of unplugging at all, especially the younger kids, the ones in elementary and middle school. They're too busy talking about video games and Godzilla. They have no perception of actual life yet. So when D.U.M.P. goes school-to-school, telling them how tempting yet misleading unplugging is, the long-term damage ear gauging would have on their health and social stature, how drastic logging off would have on their education and future lives, so many kids will hear about unplugging for the first time. They didn't even know school was optional in the first place!

By April 1, the Boycott will be seen by many, even its critics, as an undeniable success. One million people will be official recipients of the Newsletter each week, and that's not even including the private Unpluggers, the ones so off the grid they leave no paper trail. It's probably twice that number. Maybe more. Who knows? What is known is the Movement can't seem to die, despite so many outside forces desperate to end its wave of change.

If only it ended there. What a world it could've been.

7.

foundation

On April 4, 2047, Quentin will meet Esabell at Unplug's Northeastern University headquarters, and as he's ushered through the building, he'll see not only a lot of new faces, but a lot of new branding as well. He'll instantly get worried. Why doesn't he already know what's going on here? What isn't Esabell telling him?

Inside her office, Quentin will notice her desk had been moved aside, replaced with a long table with a series of cardboard displays, each propped-up on plastic holders and covered with a dramatic black cloth. "Looks like a science fair," he'll quip.

"I know we've got the Coalition meeting tomorrow," Esabell will say, closing the door behind them, "but I wanted to pitch it to everyone beforehand. It'll be easier to vote on it that way."

"What about Jax?"

"He's already on board."

Quentin will nod. "If Jax already said yes, you don't need my vote. Phibs is gonna side with the majority."

Esabell will chuckle. "I hate to break it to you, but Phibs will never vote against you."

Quentin will frown at that. "Maybe you're right."

"Besides, we *really* should be unanimous on this."

Quentin will stick his hands in his pockets. Shrug. "I'm listening."

Esabell will tense up, her nerves suddenly taking hold of her. "Alright. As you know, D.U.M.P.'s been a major road-block. It seems we're being pigeonholed as simply a Gen A thing."

"Which is to be expected."

"Yes, but—" Esabell will restrain herself, returning to her script. "In order for us to actually change the world, we're gonna have to get the parents on board too. Otherwise we'll be left with no other choice but to wait thirty years for Gen A to grow up and make Unplug the default standard of living."

Quentin will discreetly look at the row of covered displays before him, all that effort, all that planned arrangement. "That isn't so bad, you know."

"But don't you wanna live in a post-Unplug world now?"

"Of course I do, but if it doesn't happen, it doesn't happen. At least we tried."

Esabell will shake her head. "That's not how it works. We can make it happen."

"Oh really? The Millennials on both sides hate our guts."

"Yes, but we haven't done anything to deserve it. We just gotta point that out to them."

"You really think they're gonna listen?"

"If we use their kids, they will."

Quentin will stare at Esabell, an unsettling feeling brewing in his stomach.

"I mean, that's what they're doing to us, right?"

Quentin will swallow. "What did you have in mind?"

"They think they're helping their kids by forcing them back on their phones, right? But they're not."

"Of course not. They're hurting them."

"Worse." Esabell will pinch the cloth covering the first display. "They're *killing* them."

Quentin's face will go numb.

Esabell will pull the cloth away, revealing a circular logo with two childish stick figures, a parent and child. "I'm calling it 'The Happy Child Campaign.' A foundation spreading awareness about the dangers of cyberbullying, putting emphasis on the parents to encourage their kids to Unplug so they don't end up killing themselves. As good as the Boycott's been, it's a non-action system. Most people give up on non-actions and move on. This will be a way for our supporters to actually *do* something. It'll give them a real sense of contribution to a worthy cause."

Quentin's mouth will go dry, his distracted eyes darting around that simple, patronizing logo. "I'm sorry, I don't speak PR."

"Donations. Doing nothing feels good for yourself, sure, but donating to a good cause will really make people feel like they're changing the world."

"Money can't fix cyberbullying."

"No, but we could still use it to cover travel costs, advertising…" Esabell will give Quentin a subtle look. "Postage for a paper-based Newsletter."

Quentin will take a deep breath, trying to put a bright spin on it and failing.

"You have to admit, it'll solve everything."

"Why don't you just do it on your own?" Quentin will suggest. "Why does it have to be an Unplug thing?"

Esabell will furrow her brow, not expecting a rejection. "I'm sorry, but how would that look?"

"This isn't the Boycott." Quentin will pick up the Happy Child Campaign display. "This is not Unplug. This is something else."

"I know. It's the next step."

"There is no next step. The Boycott's the thing. It's the only thing. The only reason we're here."

Esabell will be stunned by Quentin's stubbornness. "I don't understand. The Internet is dangerous to children—"

"I know it is, but this… This isn't what you think it is. This is manipulation."

"Oh, and D.U.M.P. isn't?"

Quentin will place the display back on its stand. "I didn't even think about the online schools, honestly. I never went to one growing up. That's actually a legitimate thing to be concerned about."

"So are dead kids!"

"No…" Quentin will rub his eyes with both palms, trying to phrase it better. "Unplug is not a political cause. It's more than that. It's natural. Parading around with poster children… That might flip some people, sure, but it's preying on people's fears. We don't do that. We're the logical ones. Logic always wins. We don't have to sink this low."

"Children are dying—"

"They're not dying because Moms for Justice won't let their kids unplug. Christ, Esabell, we're already making them feel guilty enough. We shouldn't punish them for it."

"As it stands, the Boycott is nothing more than an alternative lifestyle. Am I wrong?"

Quentin will look away, pleading the Fifth.

"What good is that in the long run?" Esabell will ask, taking one step toward Quentin. "What change can that really bring?"

Quentin will gently unveil the remaining displays one by one. More signs. More concepts. Merch proofs. "It's voting with money."

"But the Happy Child Campaign would have the power to change *policy*. The Department of Education might actually approve in-person schools if it takes off with the Millennial parents. If that happens, we'd be in a post-Unplug world before the decade is out! Wouldn't that be fantastic?"

"I don't think the world's ready for that yet."

"They should be!"

"But they're not!" Quentin will exclaim. "It's gonna take a long time for the world to change, Esabell. We just gotta stay the course. The moment we politicalize unplugging, the more likely it's gonna burn out."

Esabell will cross her arm and scoff. "I can't believe you're actually in favor of child suicide."

"SEE!" Quentin will cry out, pointing at her. "That's what I'm talking about! That shit right there!"

"What shit?!"

"That emotional, manipulative...!" Quentin will stop, grunting a bit. "Jax approved this shit?!"

"Of course. He's been cyberbullied his whole life."

Quentin will soften. "Jax? Really?"

Esabell will nod. "He's attempted suicide twice because of it. And he sure didn't need a whole song and dance to say yes, I'll tell you that."

Quentin will instantly feel like shit. His imagination will go a bit crazy, making him sick in the process. "I... I can't believe that."

Esabell will laugh a bit. "You can't? Really? Have you *seen* the guy?"

Quentin will slowly turn his head toward her, actually appalled by her.

"Look at this one," Esabell will say, uncovering the second display, a twelve-year-old's yearbook photo. "Abcdé Meyer. A crush of hers tricked her into taking topless pics. He sent them out to a group chat. When word got back to her, she slashed her wrists."

Quentin will stare into Abcdé's sweet brown eyes.

"That was only last month." Esabell will unveil the next display, another yearbook photo, this time of a young man with a bent-up pointed nose, gaping nostrils on full display. "Greggeriee James. Fifteen. Born like that. His whole life people called him 'Pig Man.' One day his favorite teacher, Ms. Jackman, posted a meme comparing him to Porky the Pig. He shot himself with his dad's shotgun." She'll hand the photo to Quentin, revealing the next display while he's distracted, a candid photo of cute little blonde girl. "This one's the worst of them all: Khaleesi Kaputchkin. Complete strangers hounded her Instagram because of her name, bullying her over that last season of *Game of Thrones*. She jumped off a cliff."

Quentin will take Khaleesi's picture in his hand, staring deep and hard, feeling awful again. "Jesus. How old was she?"

"Eight."

"*Fuck.*"

"See? I knew you'd be on board." Esabell will gently collect the photos from Quentin, placing them back on the display table where they belong. "That's why we need this. If those moms really wanna save their kids, they need to make a big stink about cyberbullying and not the Boycott."

Quentin will bow his head apologetically. "How'd you find out about them?"

"It was a pain in the ass, believe me. Two weeks it took for us to settle on those three. We went through *thousands* of profiles, ruling out abusive parents, genetic mental illness, straight-up assholes, stuck-up bitches, school shooters, under-aged drinkers, jailbaits, anything that would make people think they kinda deserved it. Thank God we found three perfect suicides. Nothing their fault. Under sixteen. White. Relatively attractive, except for Greggeriee. And honestly, he's not even that bad. There were worse ones, believe me. His are the easiest on the eyes by far."

Quentin's face will cringe. "But don't you see how fucked up that is?"

"Of course it's fucked up. It's preventable suicide among minors."

"No, it's…" Quentin will shake his head. "It's one thing if it happened and they were the ones that inspired you to make the Happy Child Campaign in the first place. But you went *looking* for the dead kids with the most manipulative power. That's not selfless! That's not caring!"

"*Quentin*," Esabell will interrupt. "You don't speak PR. I know what I'm doing here. What do you think Rosa Parks was, the first one to do it? She wasn't. She was just the one with the lightest skin. White people were more likely to listen to her. Same thing with *Roe v. Wade*. Norma McCorvey had been selected by activists before she even *wanted* an abortion. They wanted to make abortion legal nationwide, so they picked a poor white pregnant woman from a list — just like I did — and told her to apply for an abortion, knowing she would be instantly denied. All she had to do then was carry it to term and give it up for adoption. And it worked, didn't it?

They got the circumstances they needed to bring their case to the Supreme Court. What else were they gonna do, sit around and wait for it all to happen organically? And when Michael Brown got choked out by police in Ferguson, Black Lives Matter made a big deal about it, but nothing changed. Because one could argue he was asking for it. He robbed a convenience store and struck an officer with a gun. George Floyd had to get choked out on camera seven years later over a counterfeit $20 for white people to start thinking, 'Wow, I guess Black lives really *do* matter.'"

Quentin's eyes will wander off.

"Before they switched to digital advertising, my parents were hardcore activists in their day," Esabell will say with a hint of disappointment. "You may not like it, but that's what works."

Quentin will remain silent. Deep down he'll know he can't approve the Campaign. It's a distraction, an inflammatory distraction that will only detour away from the Boycott and muddle their message. But he can't shoot it down either. Even if he can convince Phibs to vote Yes and have it passed 3-1, his No will be public record. And his followers won't be the only ones disappointed when they find out…

"Well?" Esabell will ask innocently. "What do you think?"

Quentin will look back at her. "There's no other way we can get our parents on board?"

"Not that I can think of." Esabell will pause. "And it's not just our parents. It's everyone. The last of the outliers."

Quentin will put his hands back in his pockets. After a heavy silence, he'll nod. "Alright. Let's do it."

The next day, Quentin, Jax, Esabell and Phibs will formally announce the formation of the Happy Child Campaign, the official foundation of the Unplug Movement. A proper write-up will be added to the next Newsletter, describing in detail HCC's goals and intentions, as well as the sad stories of twelve-year-old Abcdé Meyer, fifteen-year-old Greggeriee James and eight-year-old Khaleesi Kaputchkin.

When the Newsletter drops, word of the Happy Child Campaign will spread throughout Unplug circles, the parks, shopping malls, record stores, and then across social media via their Millennial parents, and then at last it'll reach every house in America. Quentin and Esabell will receive invites to talk shows and livestreams, where they'll elaborate on the dangers of cyberbullying, passing alone vital information on how viewers can donate and spread further awareness of the cause. Jax will start formal protests outside sporting events, talk shows and public parks, leading flocks of equally gauged volunteers, everyone holding up signs and chanting slogans while wearing T-Shirts with Abcdé, Greggeriee and Khaleesi's faces on them. Donations will come pouring in after that, official Unplug membership numbers soaring just as fast. Soon pins of HCC's stick figures will appear on the lapels of celebrities, news hosts, politicians and CEOs, an unspoken form of Unplug allegiance far subtler than that of a gauged earlobe, yet no less as powerful.

On June 10, 2047, the Department of Education will formally announce the dissolution of D.U.M.P. They'll send out an open letter of apology to the Unplug Movement, revealing their intention to revive nationwide in-person public education and — as a symbolic gesture — pledge the remaining $10 million of their federally assigned budget to the Happy Child Campaign.

8.

legislation

When seemingly everyone she knew was far too busy freaking out over Quentin's Manifesto during the Summer of '46, and then the Unplug Boycott the following winter, and then the Happy Child Campaign in the last few weeks of spring, Jaymeigh Grady-Smith-Waterhouse-Price had been churning out a kick-ass thesis, and she'll graduate *summa cum laude* with a perfect 4.0 GPA. To add to the joy, less than a week after she receives her Bachelors in Political Science, she'll receive word that she also managed to land her dream job: Congressional Chaperone for the House of Representatives.

The Department of Congressional Chaperones will be established in 2034, created via executive order as part of a desperate attempt to combat D.C. corruption. Since no one on Capitol Hill can seem to be trusted to do anything ethical out of their own free will, the Executive Branch had to come in and form a third-party agency of "Chaperones," one recent Poli-Sci undergrad assigned to every elected official to monitor their movements and document every word they say, their logs vetted by official auditors, to make sure everyone is followed the goddamn rules. Everyone in Congress will bitch like hell when it's first announced. It'll go to the Supreme Court, the Supreme Court will say yes, there'll be blowback... it'll be a whole thing. Nevertheless, for the sake of their reelections, everyone will eventually learn to suck it up and just be honest for a while.

Jaymeigh Grady-Smith-Waterhouse-Price will report for duty at the Department of Congressional Chaperones on July 6, 2047. To her complete and utter shock, the Representative she will be assigned to chaperone will be none other than her idol Natasha Mnozhynskyi, Ms. M herself.

Ms. M was the reason Jaymeigh wanted to get into politics in the first place. Her story was legendary, of course. Working as a waitress in New York City. Unexpectedly clinching her district's Democratic primary against a 10-term incumbent. Ultimately winning the election, making her youngest woman in Congress at that time. And she wasn't like other Representatives. She tweeted. She antagonized. She used social media as a weapon. Contested Presidents. Protested Supreme Court rulings. Painted political hashtags on her gala dresses. Doing so made Ms. M synonymous with the future. She stood out to young voters, especially young women, middle-class women, single moms especially, who wanted a great leader under the age of seventy.

Jaymeigh will try not to faint in Natasha's presence. Ms. M will be in her late fifties by 2047, but she'll still look great, fresh off her thirteenth consecutive reelection. And despite her legendary status in Jaymeigh's brain, Natasha will also be a human too. Friendly. Down to earth. Just as passionate and forthright as she was at the start. Jaymeigh will actually find herself apologizing to her for being her Congressional Chaperone, as if Ms. M would do *anything* worth snitching over. But Natasha will assure her that she felt no ill will between them, reminding Jaymeigh that she was the DCC's loudest supporter back in the day. It's only fair she be monitored like everybody else.

Two months later, on September 9, 2047, Jaymeigh will bear witness to a lunch between Natasha and Harold Cartier, a representative from Digital Tomorrow, an advocacy group representing the business interests of the largest tech companies in the country, what the Unplug Movement frequently called "The Hateful Eight." Jaymeigh will mindlessly transcribe the lunch whilst simultaneously eavesdropping out of personal curiosity.

"For the past six months, overall Internet activity has plummeted 30%," Harold will tell Natasha over their 20oz bone-in ribeyes. "Before the Happy Child Campaign, everyone thought Unplugged was just a fad my clients could squash with the right amount of cash. But now that D.U.M.P.'s gone, it seems they finally realized this Boycott might not end after all. If the worst should happen, my clients want to be assured that a post-Unplugged economic strategy is in the works that will bear their interests in mind." Harold will pull out a heavy binder and hand it over to Natasha. "We're calling it the Stable Economic Transition Act, or 'SETA' for short. It'll prevent a full-spread economic collapse thanks to the legalization of unsolicited advertising space on the outside of envelopes and packages, as well as the inside of emails."

Natasha will silently flip through the bill, her poker face unmoved.

Harold will sit up to point at the page she's on. "And as you can see on page 50, there'll be a specific set of criteria for the agencies that are legally authorized to sell such real estate."

"With Digital Tomorrow being the largest," Natasha will murmur.

"Well, naturally."

"So you're saying your clients want to profit directly from the Unplugged Movement itself?"

"This has nothing to do with their Newsletter. All postal correspondence will be affected by its passing."

Natasha will bump her brows. "Sure."

"We know it'll breeze through the Senate. The Right always sides with economic stability. But in order to win the Liberal majority in the House, we need an established Progressive backing it. Your sponsorship would give the whole thing an air of legitimacy. The Progressives will say yes, and the Moderates... Well, with your name on it, they'll it simply as the right thing to do."

Natasha will take a sip of her water, glancing briefly at Jaymeigh typing away. "I'm sorry, I'm gonna have to pass."

Harold will furrow his brow. "Natasha, I don't think you understand—"

"No, I understand you completely, Mr. Cartier," Natasha will counter, making Jaymeigh smirk. "My whole career has been in the name of radical deconstruction, punishing Conservative corruption, being the agent of change in this country." She'll shrug. "The future is Unplugged. What else is there to say?"

"You wouldn't even be here if it wasn't for the Internet," Harold will say with a hint of mockery. "It was the new medium back then, the world *you* ruled, not the Boomers. Without the Internet, you never would've been able to call out the Weinsteins and Epsteins in power. You never would've been able to side with the desert nation of your choice or whatever former Soviet state was most in need of your help. Are you really going to let a bunch of entitled Gen A babies take that away from you?"

Natasha will stare for effect. "Those *babies* are scaring the shit out of your clients, Mr. Cartier. They're not underestimating them. Neither should you." She'll stand and look at Jaymeigh. "I think we're done here."

Harold will watch in shock as Natasha and Jaymeigh leave the restaurant with barely restrained jubilation.

That night Natasha's phone will ring, waking her up. She'll remove her sleep mask, cursing the fates as she grabs her cell phone. "You have any idea what fucking time it is?" she'll ask whoever's on the line.

"Is your new Chaperone still there?" Douglas Cameron will ask, swirling brandy in his living room four blocks away.

Natasha will open her eyes. Slide up. Turn her bedside lamp on. "No. Of course not."

"Good." Cameron will sip his snifter. "Heard you met with Cartier today."

"How'd you hear that?"

"I have a Chaperone too, Natasha. You know they like to gossip."

"Not Jaymeigh. She's one of the good ones."

"Mine too."

"Oh yeah? What's she good at?"

Cameron will scoff. "Hacking."

"Get to the point, Doug. I'm tired."

"Gladly." Cameron will sip some more. "Call Harold back. Tell him you'll sponsor SETA after all."

"You're not changing my mind on that."

"Can't hate me for trying."

"You want it passed so badly? You sponsor it."

"I can't. I've already turned them down."

Natasha will hesitate. "You did?"

"I was their first choice. Thanks to those drunk tweets of mine, I've made myself synonymous with Unplugged hate."

"Why would you say no then?"

"I want to get reelected, same as you."

"That wasn't my reason."

"On the record, sure. Showing off for the new girl, are we?"

"I meant what I said."

"You're not getting too attached to her, are you?"

Natasha will frown at that. "There's nothing wrong with a friend."

"Oh my God, you're such a *Messiah!*"

"I never used that word."

"Don't lie, Natasha. You haven't changed. Flaunting for the headlines. Meeting-and-greeting for fun when it wasn't an election year. I know how much you love having a little fucking acolyte follow you around, singing your praises, worshiping the ground you step on."

Natasha will huff. "Heard you're going for the Presidency."

Cameron will grin. "Now how'd you hear about that?"

"Jaymeigh's good."

"Good at what?"

"Hearing. Reporting both ways." Natasha will pause. "So it's true then?"

Cameron will shrug. "I'm trying at least. Hard to fight a staunch stance I've already blasted all over Twitter."

"Yeah, good luck with that."

"SETA needs to happen, Natasha. Presidency or not, it'll never pass with me behind it. It's predictable. Of course Douglas Cameron wants it. But Ms. M? Maybe that means there's something there worth exploring."

Natasha will shake her head slowly. "I'm not bailing out Big Internet. They milked the shit out of those kids for decades. They had their fun. Now they can vote and they're voting with their money. Good for them."

"It's not a bailout, Natasha. It's a white flag. They're giving up. They know they can't win against the inevitable. The richer they get alongside Unplugged, the happier we'll all be in the end."

"What does that mean?"

"You know they've got their hands on everyone."

"Not me, apparently."

"How about this…" Cameron will pause. "If you get SETA passed, I'll make it my personal mission to make you Speaker."

Natasha's heart will stop. "Bullshit."

"The Internet and the economy are too intertwined. A boycott would be devastating for everyone. You know it. I know it. The ISPs know it. Most importantly, the voters know it. And they'll blame the President, which I will be. I will make you Speaker, Natasha. I swear on my kids I will."

Natasha's heart will be racing. "I'm gonna have to tell all this to Jaymeigh, you know."

"I figured that."

Natasha will nod to herself. "I'll let you know tomorrow."

"I look forward to hearing from you." Cameron will hang up.

Natasha will hang her head over her desk the next morning, both hands holding up her neck. She'll sigh and look up at Jaymeigh.

Jaymeigh won't know what to say at first. She'll lick her lips, trying to process under pressure. "What do you think about it?"

Natasha will half-shrug. "There was always something in the way before. This is an actual guarantee, Jaymeigh. Speaker of the House! Why shouldn't I do it?"

Jaymeigh will nod halfheartedly.

That won't be enough for Natasha. "Tell me."

"Tell you what?"

"What do you think?"

Jaymeigh will hesitate. "I'm just a Chaperone. It's not my place to have an opinion."

Natasha will shake her head a little. "You're more than that."

"I wasn't assigned to you because I wrote a thesis on you. I was made a Chaperone because a Congressional committee determined that I routinely avoid letting bias cloud my judgment."

Natasha will sit up. "You really are one of the good ones."

"Thank you, ma'am."

Natasha will study Jaymeigh's serious expression. "What if next time…" She'll pause, her eyes on her desk. "What if next time they say I'm too old? Or too bitchy? Too bossy?"

Jaymeigh will refuse to emote, her face hard as stone.

Natasha will nod nonetheless. "I can do so much more as Speaker, Jaymeigh. I've put in thirty years. I'm ready."

Jaymeigh will grab her purse. "I'm gonna powder my nose if it's okay."

"I'll be here," Natasha will murmur.

Jaymeigh will stand. Open the door. Stop. Look back at Natasha. "Off the record… I think you'd make a *fantastic* Speaker."

Natasha will find herself overwhelmed with emotion, unable to suppress her relief and joy.

Jaymeigh will throw in a smile and close the door. She will then take her time to the bathroom as she grapples with the sobering reality check that the sparkling Ms. M, the Progressive Queen of Capitol Hill, might just be, in fact, exactly like everyone else.

9.

riot

Natasha Mnozhynskyi will introduce SETA on the House floor two days later to little-to-no fanfare. A few days later, however, a copy of SETA will find its way in the hands of *The Washington Post*. They'll nickname it "Natasha's Bill" and wait for a particularly slow news day in October to leak it.

The Unplug Movement will be in an uproar about it. Quentin Wagner himself will call a press conference to angrily, vehemently condemn the greedy Hateful Eight for such a blatant invasion of privacy and violation of human rights. The transcript of his rambling speech will be printed in every Unplug Newsletter. For Esabell and Phibs, that'll be enough to settle the issue of Natasha's Bill, but not Jax. He won't just be pissed off about it. He'll be downright *disturbed*. It needed to be killed. Everyone that allowed it to exist needed to be publicly outed, voted out and boycotted for life. It was so obviously wrong. He can't let them get away with that.

In the weeks that follow, Jax will divert his network of picketers away from Happy Child Campaign rhetoric and instead protest Natasha's Bill. One particularly nasty demonstration will occur outside *The Morning Show*, Jax leading a crowd of equally angry Unpluggers in a spit-a-thon on the glass behind the hosts, a disgusting image that will go viral on Twitter before stream's end.

Many media organizations will conflate the two issues under attack by the Unplugged Movement, cyberbullying and Natasha's Bill, getting their wires crossed in the process. Every once in a while, during a free hour of improvised speculating, a commentator will verbalize the common misconception: the Hateful Eight wants to pass Natasha's Bill so they can (somehow?) profit from dead kids. Other news outlets, particularly the ones directly owned by the Hateful Eight, will use said confusing conflation as further evidence of Unplugged's disorganization and stupidity.

Natasha herself will receive concentrated backlash from the underground Unplug punk scene, particularly through a grungy cover of Dolly Parton's "Jolene" retitled "Ms. M." Also notable will be an extended rewrite of Pink Floyd's "Pigs (Three Different Ones)," Natasha being the focus of the second verse just so the lead singer can call her a "fucked up old hag." (Oddly enough, despite clocking in at fifteen minutes, the "Pigs" cover will reach number 4 on the *Billboard* Hot 100.)

Despite all of this, Natasha herself will remain incredibly ambivalent toward the Unplug Movement. She expected some blowback in her sponsoring the bill, sure. That's what happens when you're in Washington. Nothing's gonna change her mind regarding SETA. The economy had built itself on the backs of digital technology. Mending the transition would be the wisest decision for the future of America. And she merely sponsored it; she didn't write the damn thing. She's not personally profiting off of dead kids or Millennial greed. She's just the voice of the Progressives. When she tweets, people listen. She sets the tone for her party.

But no one will give a fig about Natasha's Bill after October 21, 2047. Because something more important will happen. Something awful.

It was supposed to be a simple park protest. Jax and his two "generals" Munt and Bro (their real legal names) had flown out to Los Angeles to lead a camp-out in Plaza Park. The protesters got a little rowdy by hour four, and a small pack of demonstrators, some two dozen, somehow split off and made their way to the nearby YouTube Theater, where the 2047 MTV Video Music Awards were about to begin. That pack of protesters, headed by a vigilant brute named Lossy (also his real legal name), was stopped at the red carpet by security. A punch was thrown. Steel fences were tossed. A fight broke out. Celebrities got smacked by signs and punching fists. The police showed up in riot gear, forcing Lossy's protesters to retreat *into* YouTube Theater, completely disrupting the ceremony. A hostage crisis dragged on for hours, all livestreamed for the world to see. What a complete shitshow.

Ultimately no one was killed or seriously injured in what'll be forever known as the VMA Riots, the worse casualties being a security guard's black eye and Lossy himself getting banged up a bit at the end there. But the ISP-controlled media, now in the driver's seat for the first time in months, will oversaturate the news cycle with coverage, spinning what was otherwise an isolated incident as "the REAL Unplugged movement," grown men and women going "You see?! You SEE?! We told you!" for far too many hours.

Jax will return to Boston the next day, his flip phone ringing the moment his plane landed at Logan International. An emergency Coalition meeting had been called at its usual venue, the basement of Park Street Church.

Jax will arrive twenty minutes late to find Quentin, Esabell and Phibs waiting for him with a document on the table, an open letter to the Unplug Movement vehemently condemning the VMA Riots. The others had already signed it.

"I'm not signing that," Jax will declare, shocking everyone. "I saw Lossy in the hospital. I *thanked him* for his initiative. I'm not turning my back on those that want to take our cause in their own hands."

"What the fuck is wrong with you?!" Quentin will holler. "This is a disaster! If we're not all in agreement on this, it'll look like Unplug condones violence!"

"Who says we don't condone violence?"

"SIGN THE FUCKING LETTER!" Quentin will scream back, no shame in how he looked to Phibs and Esabell.

"Is this a revolution or isn't it?!"

"Sign the fucking letter! If you don't, everything we've built up to this point will be GONE! This will set us back YEARS!"

"WHO CARES?!" Jax will shout back. "They can't pass that bill, Quentin! They can't make money off us! They don't get to adapt! They fucking RUINED us! They hurt us and beat the shit out of us!"

Quentin will let out hard, mocking cackles. "Really? Your Internet Service Provider beat the shit out of you?"

"Yeah, actually. *Motherfucker.* Yeah, he did." Jax will scowl, his blood boiling. "You've never been in a fucking fight, have you? You've never had your face plastered around for people to mock. Constantly getting shit on. Feeling like absolute garbage, only to come home and get shit on some more and smacked around for no reason. Okay?"

Quentin will stand there, speechless.

Jax will rub the back of his head, eyes puffy, cheeks red. "I know you're great with words. That's alright. That's your thing. This is mine. This is my field, and *believe me*, just lying down and taking it won't change a damn thing."

"But hurting other people will? Scaring people? Fighting with fists because we hit a little snag?"

"That bill goes against the Boycott! It goes against the Manifesto! It goes against the Charter! The Coalition! It goes against EVERYTHING we stand for!"

"I agree. But there are legal options. Mature, adult options we can use. We can't get violent on a moment's notice and expect anyone to listen to us. How can you not see that?"

Jax will shrug. "So we're just gonna let the Hateful Eight save their corporate asses?"

"As long as the Internet stops being the default in the process, yeah. That's the fucking point, Jax. I didn't forget that."

"And I have?"

"Yeah." Quentin will frown. "Yeah, I guess you have." He'll sit back down. Look away with disappointment.

Jax will stare, genuinely hurt by Quentin's disapproval. "We used to take our frustrations out in words, you know. Just like you did. Little comments. Little tweets. TrueSwitch rants. Videos in our car. That used to be enough. That's how we got it out of our system, but we can't anymore, can we?"

Quentin won't know how to respond to that.

Jax will scoff. "What do you think? You think that little piece of paper's gonna stop all this from happening again? What's the next one gonna say, huh? What are you going to SAY when everyone stops throwing hands and starts throwing bricks, huh?! Huh?! C'mon, O Wise One, what are you gonna SAY?!" He'll storm out in frustration.

To avoid drawing unnecessary attention to the absence of Jax's signature, Quentin will release the open letter on October 23rd with only his signature on it, spinning it as him choosing to represent Unplug as a whole. But the letter will fall on deaf ears, the media having already made its mind up on the matter.

Cal Vectors will feel the egg on his face when Gabe, Flora, and the rest of his brother's content creator friends tease him about those damn Unpluggers at the VMAs. Even Jim will have a hard time defending his brother's Pro-Unplug stance.

But Cal will try to explain anyway: "I actually *don't* side with the rioters. I've always been against violence. They shouldn't have done it. That doesn't mean they're wrong about the Internet. I see good Unpluggers every day. I know they're better than that. And Quentin condemned the riots. He said those people didn't represent the Movement, and I believe him. Anyone who uses Unplug as an excuse to scare people and hurt people are just stupid morons who don't understand nuance."

"So you *are* against them?" Gabe will ask.

And Cal will groan, murmuring, "No, Gabe, I'm not. Unplug the philosophy is okay. It's Unplug the *organization* I have some qualms about."

Gabe will chortle and say, "What's the difference?"

And Cal will feel lonely again, privately bearing his feelings of betrayal. Those guys were already in the right. Why'd they have to go and make things so complicated?

Natasha Mnozhynskyi's ambivalence toward the Unplug Movement will explode the same time the front of her house does, the day before Halloween. She won't remember any of it, only that she was making a sandwich around 11 PM on the first floor of her D.C. townhouse, minding her own business, when a flash of light and blast of smoke knocked her back and she hit her head.

The police will succeed in capturing the lone assailant, a verified Unplugger from Delaware named Sprite McGinty, seventeen years old. In the interrogation room, Sprite will go off on how he concocted the plan to kill Natasha when a bunch of pals told him how much of a monster she was, how she claimed to be a so-called ally despite selling out the movement to the enemy, how she probably masturbated to mental pictures of dead cyberbullied teens, shoving all that lobbyist kickback money up her twat (a seventeen-year-old will really say all that, scaring even the detectives interrogating him), and that the only way to stop Natasha's Bill from passing was to kill Natasha herself.

A recording of Sprite McGinty's twisted, unapologetic confession will somehow find itself in the hands of the media and, of course, get all blown out of proportion.

Quentin will learn about Ms. M's assassination attempt from Phibs. His first reaction will be that of sorrow, sorrow for the damage his Movement had already inflicted on the world, and he'll fuel that sorrow into a statement of condolence to Natasha Mnozhynskyi, wishing her a speedy recovery, adding a further condemnation to any violent-minded Unpluggers still out there.

Later that night, after Phibs clocks out for the night, Quentin will sit in his dark office and stare at his landline phone, dwelling on Sprite McGinty's words, how familiar they sounded. After a few moments of second guessing, he'll pick up the receiver and make a long-distance call to D.C. Police.

Instead of waiting around the hospital for a copycat crime to occur, Natasha Mnozhynskyi will transfer her care to Jaymeigh's apartment, where the Chaperone lived alone.

There, the two women will bond in ways they never had before.

"I'm kinda glad it happened," Natasha will tell Jaymeigh one night over a bottle of wine.

"You do?"

"Now I know what I'm up against." Natasha will refill her glass. "I don't know why I keep defending them. They don't care about a better future. They just wanna fuck shit up for kicks."

Jaymeigh will hesitate, trying to keep her unease down. "I'm sure that's not true."

"They don't care about the economy. They don't care about human lives. All that Happy Child bullshit's a fucking lie. Believe me, I've seen it a thousand times. Anyone who actually falls for that shit is just as backwards and stupid as Unpluggers themselves."

And Jaymeigh will listen to Natasha go on and on, trying her best to reserve judgment, but she'll find herself quite horrified by that other side of Ms. M. Jaymeigh knew quite a few Unpluggers herself, all of them smart, decent people quite capable of critical thinking and self-awareness, not stupid or backward at all. In fact, Jaymeigh herself was a closeted Unplugger, believing the pros of the argument to greatly outweigh the cons. How can someone she admired so much, not just as a politician but as a woman as well, be so short-sighted and judgmental, just like those Conservatives she spent her entire career crusading against?

In the weeks following Ms. M's assassination attempt, major corporations will announce one-by-one that they're banning Unplug members from entering their establishment out of safety concerns, something easy to enforce thanks to their easily identifiable gauged ears. Companies that will implement an Unplug ban include Best Buy, RadioShack, GameStop, Starbucks, Dunkin', Regal Cinemas, AMC Theatres, Olive Garden, Applebee's, CVS, Walgreen's, Dick's Sporting Goods, BJ's, Costco and Barnes & Noble. Such a gesture might seem like a heavy blow to the Unplug Movement, but in actuality many Unpluggers will have already switched to Mom & Pop alternatives by then. The Unplug ban will really be for everyone else, the vehemently anti-Unplugged, a way for them to feel safe out and about despite no actual threat of danger, a last-ditch effort from the declining franchises to gain just a little bit more business.

Equally meaningless will be the Unplug counter-ban, Mom & Pop businesses openly discouraging anyone who isn't a supporter of Unplug from using their establishments, a way for them to publicly voice their support for the unjustly judged Unpluggers, the ones that did everything right and yet were openly discriminated for simply having gaps in their earlobes, let alone dreams of a more humane future, one without algorithms and suffocation, without dead kids and addicted elders.

One organization that will take such solidarity a step too far will be Austin's Prudential Movie House, Cal Vector's place of employment.

Cal will clock in to find his manager Mr. G waiting for him with unusual nervousness. "Cal, can I talk to you for a sec?"

Cal will follow Mr. G into his office. "What is it?"

Mr. G will sit on the edge of his desk. "I need you to gauge your ears."

Cal will chuckle. "God, you made me think I was getting fired."

"I'm going to the mall now. That way we can make it back before the 10:30 crowd gets here."

"Wait, why?" Cal will blink. "I don't have to, do I?"

Mr. G will hesitate. "Cal..."

"I'm fine. Thanks."

"If they come in and see your ears looking like that..."

"They'll what?" Cal will snap. "C'mon, they already know I'm with them."

"But what about the ones that don't know you?"

"Who cares?"

"It's just a simple procedure. It's not gonna hurt."

"I don't care if it hurts or not. It's not real. It's just for show."

"You support Unplug, don't you?"

Cal will stare. "Of course I do. How can you ask me that?"

"Then what's the problem? Just gauge your ears."

Cal will chuckle some more. "Well, three things actually. I don't believe in piercings or tattoos. Never did."

Mr. G will shrug. "So?"

"Second, the only reason they gauge their ears in the first place is because Quentin hole-punched his ear in front of a crowd, and I don't even know if I believe that. But even if he did do it, going to the mall and getting a sanitized copy under sterile conditions is not the same thing. Not even close."

Mr. G will only sigh at that.

"And last..." Cal will cross his arms. "I prefer to pick and choose how much of an Unplugger I am. I'm against violence for one, and if suddenly the Unplug Movement condoned violence under certain conditions, I don't want to be confused with the ones that support that."

Mr. G will shake his head. "You have to do it, Cal."

"You're gonna fire me over this?"

"Don't put me in that position."

Cal's heart will jump. "What do you mean?"

"You know I don't want to, Cal," Mr. G will say softly. "It's not personal. It's just bad for business."

"This whole thing has been bad for business!" Cal will cry, full-on panicking now. "This place was never about the money! It was supposed to be about the fucking movies!"

"Not anymore. I need a team player now, and if you're not doing this with me, I'm afraid you're gonna have to go."

"Even though it's objectively stupid?"

"The customer's always right. If they don't feel safe here, they'll go somewhere else."

Cal will shake his head. "Mr. G..."

"It's not gonna hurt."

"Stop saying that!" Cal will yell. "I've been a team player for the past twenty-five years, Mr. G! This is my only job! I don't have anything else!"

"You're really gonna throw it away over a couple of gauged ears?"

Cal will feel tears coming on. "Well… if it's the only thing standing between you trusting me and not, then I'm afraid I'm gonna have to quit."

Mr. G will roll his eyes. "God, why do you have to make it so complicated?"

"You're the one! I shouldn't have to prove my loyalty to you! I defended this place when everyone was shitting on it! When everyone said it was too old or dirty or expensive! I even defended *them* when no one thought an Unplugged world was possible! When Quentin said the riots didn't represent the Movement, I passed that message along the best I could! I have always been on their side! Why isn't that enough?!" Cal will pause, trying to catch his breath. "The bans are stupid and phony anyway! Why are you playing into all that?!"

Mr. G will check his watch. "I don't have time for this. Come with me or don't." Mr. G will walk past a distraught Cal, taking his time down the street toward the mall.

But Cal won't follow Mr. G. With bile in his throat and tears in his eyes, Cal will frown one last goodbye at that lovely old Movie House before walking out the door and heading home.

10.

thanksgiving

Jax Halsteder will spend Thanksgiving at Unplug's MIT headquarters, stressed out his mind, arguing with Bro and Lossy over how they can bail Munt out of jail. He knows Quentin has $50,000 to spare, but how are they gonna get him to loan them the money without telling him what Munt did to get himself arrested in the first place?

A loud knock will interrupt their conversation. Jax will whip the door open, primed to attack whoever it was, and freeze at the familiar face before him.

"Hey, Son," Benjamin Halsteder will say with a genuine smile. Balding head. Pock marks on his face. Horrible teeth. Otherwise a spitting image of Jax.

Jax will awkwardly look at Bro and Lossy, their faces naturally suspicious at the Millennial standing at the door. "I'm in the middle of something," Jax will mumble, trying to close the door. Benjamin will naturally stop it with a strong grab, triggering Jax with violent memories past.

But Benjamin will relax, lowering his hand with ashamed self-awareness. "I... I just wanted to see you. You haven't been home in a while."

"I really can't talk."

"Please."

"Get out." Jax will slam the door and resume his conversation with Bro and Lossy, completely unfazed by the events that just transpired.

Thirty minutes later, Jax, Bro and Lossy will reemerge from the office with a battle plan on how to break the news to Quentin at the next Coalition meeting. Jax will be halfway across the recruitment center when he'll halt at the sight of his father still in the building, filling out paperwork, politely asking questions to Lip West, one of Jax's recruiters. "What the FUCK do you think you're doing?!" Jax will shout across the room, storming up to his father.

Benjamin will actually be intimidated. "I'm becoming a member."

"THIS IS NOT FOR YOU!" Jax will smack the clipboard out of his father's hands, silencing the entire headquarters.

Hundreds of recruiters and new members will stop what they're doing and watch, scared stiff at the sight.

"YOU CAN'T JUST SHOW UP HERE AND FORCE YOURSELF IN!" Jax will scream at Benjamin.

Benjamin will frown, genuinely hurt by his son's outburst. He'll bend down and pick up the clipboard, gently handing it back to Lip.

"Thank you," Lip will say with an embarrassed smile.

"DON'T *THANK* HIM!" Jax will yell at Lip.

"I just…" Benjamin will swallow. "I'm just so proud of you, Son. You're fighting the fuckers that took my job and gave it to a computer—"

"That's not why," Jax will grumble.

"Nevertheless." Benjamin will gaze at Jax softly. "We have something in common now. We can build on that."

"Lossy," Jax will mutter, stepping aside, refusing to look at Lossy wrangling Benjamin out of the headquarters. Lossy will even get the opportunity to smack the Millennial around a bit before tossing him to the curb.

That night, college-aged Unpluggers will return to their Anti-Unplug households, the generation gap between them and their parents now a colossal gulf. But despite what the ISP-controlled media will report in advance, the Unpluggers will not be wielding knives of war at the table, waiting to pounce when their trap has sprung. And despite what the editorial section of the official Unplug Newsletter will warn in advance, their Millennial parents won't use the dinner as an excuse to aggressively nullify their "radical" children. In fact, both parties will be motivated by the same forces: love and disappointment.

Unpluggers will lament how little their parents understand their decision to boycott, truly wishing they could share their newfound epiphany with their family. And the Millennials will simply be scared, desperate to understand why their kids feel the way they do about their upbringing, just wanting to make it clear that they want to remain a part of their lives, no matter what they believe in. That's not to say both sides won't feel pressure to convert the ignorant toward illumination; they will. But both sides will also be aware of how tense the conversation can get, and they'll try to abate it as much as they can.

Sadly, the whole thing will end in disaster for everyone. No matter how the conversation starts, which side was the one to speak first, it'll all end the same way. Millennials naturally scoffing at their children's accusations that it was wrong to give them tablets so young, to use social media in front of them, how backwards they'd be if they kept on resisting the inevitable. And the Unpluggers will be incensed by their parents' juvenile concern for their well-being, believing any visit to a shopping mall or a movie theater to be just two steps away from a full-blown riot. All good intentions will be trumped by months and months of media pre-programming, one side figuring out the other side's point long before their sentence is even finished, just from how they started it. It can even be set off with the simple use of the wrong buzzword. "Unplugged" instead of "Unplug." "Riot" instead of "demonstration." "Brainwashed" at any given time.

All the Thanksgiving dinners that year will end the same way, in tears, all because of a simple misunderstanding of motives. To each side it'll feel so personal, like their entire world had ended, theirs and no one else's. That is why Thanksgiving 2047 will forever be immortalized — by both sides — as "the Thanksgiving from Hell."

Esabell Cortina-Gomez will have a slightly different experience than the standard Unplug Thanksgiving. Her parents weren't simpletons behind on the times like everyone else. They knew everything about institutional activism. They knew the game, they saw it all, so any resistance to the Unplug Movement won't be from a place of ignorance. She actually thought going in that her family's Thanksgiving would be the exception.

"Crime rates will go up without the Internet," Javier Cortina will scold her over turkey, candied sweet potatoes and croissants. "Corrupt politicians will get away with more, knowing no one has the voice to stop them."

"Not to mention the widespread distribution of news will vanish overnight," Elizabeth Gomez will add. "That'll affect developing nations the most."

"Your mother's right. The Internet isn't just America, you know. It's the whole world. And the first-world problems of a nation should not be solved at the detriment of the impoverished and disenfranchised."

Esabell will be appalled by her parents' words. Of all the people not to understand the point of the Unplug Movement, she never thought her parents to be among them. And she'll unleash stern words at her former idols, those phony role models, the ones she thought she could look up to all her life, being proud of their achievements, what they had fought for, to criticize them for *their* complacency.

"You let it get this bad!" she'll proclaim. "You knew how damaging social media was on mental health, on body image! You knew the damage screen addiction had on the human body! And then you went and gave tablets and smartphones to KIDS?! Children?! Even though social media companies intentionally boosted incendiary content! Even though widespread fraud stole thousands of dollars from gullible senior citizens with no way to track it down or get it back! Even with all that Internet-based journalism focusing more on clickbait headlines and outrage stories, distorting reality day after day just to make a few extra bucks, flowing all that anger and cynicism and political extremism into our pockets, into our brains! You knew it was all bad! You knew and you did NOTHING!"

"We did everything we could!" Elizabeth will cry at her. "How can you say we did nothing?!"

"Because it's still here! It's bigger than ever now! They're even trying to get a bill passed to keep the economy from crashing because of us! That's how big you let it get! You could've done this years ago without any risk of financial danger or long-term social repercussions, but you didn't!"

"You don't understand," Javier will plead. "No one had a problem with the Internet back then. Were people abusing it? Of course they were. But we figured out a way to coexist with it, just like everyone else."

"Oh, but sexual assault, mental health days, safe spaces, microaggressions, that all had to be treated with the utmost nuance and sensitivity, no exceptions. Why not this, huh? Why weren't you as angry about this?"

"Esabell—"

"NO, Dad! Admit it! You fucking gave up! And no wonder, you guys own everything now! Now YOU'RE the ones making the money at OUR detriment! Of course you'd want to keep everything exactly the same! How FUCKING convenient!"

"That's not why!" Elizabeth will insist. "We didn't give up!" She'll let out desperate sigh. "I guess we just… mellowed out."

Esabell will cringe at those two words: "*Mellowed out?*"

"It happens to everyone," Javier will say.

"You'll see," Elizabeth will add. "When you give everything to something and it gets taken away from you, you think you can just fight on, but… It's just not the same the second time. And when it keeps happening again, you just can't do it anymore. And then we had you, and the world didn't seem so bad anymore, and—"

"That's not gonna be me!" Esabell will declare. "I swear to God, I'm gonna fix this mess you and your entire FUCKING generation made for us! I'm not gonna *mellow out* when the going gets tough! You just fucking watch!"

Javier will stare at her with dead eyes. "Yes, you will."

"We never thought it'd happen to us," Elizabeth will say, completely exhausted. "But it did."

Esabell will fight through her doubts. "Well, that's just cause you're weak. I'm not. Watch me." And she'll storm up to her room.

Cal Vectors will spend Thanksgiving alone, eating a TV dinner in front of his TV. His brother Jim had invited him over to his house again, promising those assholes from last year weren't there out of respect for Cal losing his job, but Cal will leave all those texts on read. Mr. G's texts too. How dare he try to make it up to him. Too little too late.

But Cal won't blame Mr. G for what happened. It wasn't his fault. Not really. It was them. The Unplugged. Quentin and Jax and Esabell and Phibs. All of them. Those punks at the theater, Gozer and Zuul. All of them on the street. Everywhere. It's their fault. He had one good thing in his life and they took it away from him, despite everything he did for them.

And the TV will parrot his resentment. He'll catch a *Law & Order* about a homicidal Unplugger. During the climatic interrogation scene, the suspect will break down in tears, reverting back to the kid he really is, admitting he was just blindly following his friends when he broke those windows, threw that tear gas and murdered under orders. And Cal will eat his Hungry Man feeling validated, knowing firsthand how childish and immature those Unplugged are, hating Quentin for making unplugging possible in the first place, forcing it on everyone.

He'll spend entire hours hating them. TV would be gone too if it were up to them, wouldn't it? Replaced by paper written by them. Complete brain control. Ruling a world where it's okay to fire people and distrust people if they aren't using the correct buzzwords or have normal un-gauged ears.

Natasha Mnozhynskyi will be hosting a Thanksgiving of her own inside Jaymeigh Grady-Smith-Waterhouse-Price's quaint little apartment, sitting at a table set for three.

"I'll try her again," Natasha will mumble, putting her phone back to her ear.

Jaymeigh will finish off their bottle of wine, their dinners already done, the third plate fully loaded with ice-cold food. "It's okay if she—"

"She'll be here." Natasha will clear her throat just before Iverna's voicemail began. "Hey honey. Don't know if you got my messages, but I'm here at Jaymeigh's waiting for you. We can always reheat your food. Oh, just in case you didn't get the email, the address is 325 Ma—" A knock on the door. "Oh, I think that's you now! Bye!" Natasha will hang up. "Oh God."

"I'll get it." Jaymeigh will stand up and open the door, revealing a twenty-one-year-old with messy blonde hair, hot pink gauges, a patched-up denim jacket, a black leather skirt, and a matching pair of dommy mommy stompers.

"I guess you're Jaymeigh," Iverna Mnozhynskyi will mumble dismissively.

"Hey!" Natasha will call out, standing up with a girly grin. "You're here!"

"Yeah, cause you won't stop calling me."

"Come on in," Jaymeigh will say, gesturing behind her.

Iverna will hold up a hand. "No way. It's already bad enough having a dead-kid-loving bitch of a mom. I'm not going anywhere near her."

Natasha's face will crumble. Her knees will give out as she plops back into her chair.

"Your mom just got attacked, alright?" Jaymeigh will snarl at Iverna. "Cut her some slack."

Iverna will shrug. "She looks fine to me."

"Well she's not, alright? She pretends for your sake, but more than anything she just wanted to spend Thanksgiving with her daughter."

Iverna will scoff. "Don't pretend you know anything about her."

"All she did was sponsor a bill, alright? That's her duty as a Congresswoman."

"Chill your britches, bitch."

"Don't you TALK LIKE THAT TO HER!" Natasha will shout.

"I'll talk to her however the FUCK I want!" Iverna will shout back. She'll look at Jaymeigh. "You wanna know what my mom's really like? She doesn't care about you. Even after what she just said, she doesn't care about you. If you weren't here right now, she wouldn't have invited me over for Thanksgiving. She's just adjusting for her audience. Always has, always will. You think she's a feminist?" Iverna will laugh. "Oh no, she hates women. Blacks too. Jews. Palestinians. Gays. All of 'em. But suddenly she gets a chance to nab a Congressional seat, so what does she do? She plays the perfect ally. She loved playing that gender card when it suited her. The middle-class card. But that's not what made her exceptional. No, what made her *exceptional* was playing the role of the angry young Internet-savvy Democrat, the one she knew every angry young Internet-savvy Democrat would vote for blindly, cause she's *just like them.* I'm sure it was hard at first, keeping up a façade like that, but she got the hang of it. If she was the one that declared what times were ending and for whom, she'd live forever. Do you really think she'd throw away the Internet, her playground, for the sake of the country's well-being? No way." Iverna will stare at her mom, that weak Fascist pretending to be upset. "Because she's nothing and nobody without it."

Natasha will frown down at her plate.

Iverna will look at Jaymeigh. "What'd they promise her? Speaker?"

Jaymeigh will say nothing.

"Figures." Iverna will shake her head at Natasha. "You stupid fool." She'll pivot and stroll down the hall.

Jaymeigh will slowly close the door and glance over at the numb Natasha sitting at her dinner table. And she'll feel bad for her own feelings against her. Natasha might not be the Progressive Jesus she thought she was, but she certainly wasn't Judas either. And she didn't deserve any condemnation from anyone.

Quentin will be sitting in his office after hours, planning to stay there for Thanksgiving, when he'll suddenly feel a pang he hadn't felt in a while.

Opening the office door, he'll be shocked to find Phibs still sitting at his desk. "What are you doing here?" he'll ask with a stoic face.

"I didn't want you to be alone for Thanksgiving," Phibs will answer meekly.

Quentin will simply give a distracted nod. "I think I wanna go to Danvers after all. Surprise my dads. I'm feeling homesick, I think."

"That sounds nice."

Quentin will shrug. "Wanna come with me?"

Phibs will grin. "Yeah," he'll say with a chuckle. "Sounds like fun."

Daddy and I will just be lifting our forks when we hear the doorbell ring. I'll get up to answer it and practically squeal at the sight of my son, my Quentin, and I'll bring him in for a big, tight hug, trying my hardest not to cry. After so many years, seeing my son again… I'll be beside myself. And his ears will be gauged, just like I knew they'd be, but the one on his right will be significantly misshapen. And I'll notice he had someone with him, another young man with gauged ears, but Quentin will read my mind and quickly define him as just a friend. "Amphibian," apparently. Phibs for short. What a stupid name. But he'll be so nice, that Phibs. What a good friend for Quentin.

Daddy and Phibs will do most of the talking at dinner. Quentin and I will occasionally make eye contact before we instantly divert them away. How alike we'll both be by then. He won't be as thin as the last time I saw him, collecting his diploma on the Emerson stage. He'll be cleaner. Healthier. And I'll be so proud of how... what's the word... *professional* he'll be. Not that he wasn't professional before. Not at all. He's just... Oh, I'll be so happy I won't even care what he is or isn't. He's home. My baby boy is home.

I'll get up to make coffee for everyone just as Quentin gets a phone call. He'll excuse himself from the table and take it outside, as cold as it is out there. I'll discreetly watch him through the window as I fill the pot with water. I'll see that change on his face. Definitely bad news. And after Quentin lets himself back in, sitting next to that friend of his with the funny name, he'll pretend like nothing's happened. But Daddy will notice the change in him too. He'll ask what's wrong. Phibs too, he'll ask what's wrong. But Quentin will just shrug it off. "You'll find out tomorrow," he'll murmur to Phibs.

"What's tomorrow?" his Daddy will ask.

But Quentin will say nothing, growing cold and withdrawn. Phibs will fill the void with a happy explanation of how their Coalition works, their biweekly meetings, the inner workings of the Movement and all that, but I won't be paying as much attention as Quentin's Daddy. I'll only be focused on my son. That sadness in his eyes. That sudden change. It'll just break my heart.

We'll finish watching *Planes, Trains & Automobiles* around 10. Quentin will excuse himself and sit on the back porch step. I'll sneak over to the home bar, pour out two snifters of Courvoisier VSOP, and slide the back door open to join him.

"I want to be alone," he'll grumble.

But I'll slide the door shut and sit beside him anyway, holding out his snifter. "I haven't seen you in almost a decade. You're drinking with me."

Quentin will begrudgingly take the cognac with a sigh.

I'll take a sip of mine, trying to get the ball rolling. "We've been following you guys ever since *The Evening Show*."

"Is that right?"

"I just wanted the opportunity to tell you, in person, how proud we both are of you."

And Quentin won't know what to say to that. He'll swirl his snifter and sip, smacking his lips a bit. "Thank you. Means a lot."

And I'll smile a bit, thinking back. "You're so much like me. I used to listen to 40s music back in Middle School. All the hits back then were about strippers, binge-drinking and drugs. I was such a prude back then. But I really did love it, the way it used to be. And that definition changed as I grew older. 50s. 60s. 70s. *Even* the 80s. And yet it was always still the same: the way it used it be." I'll sip some more. "And now you're the same way. Amazing how much we get from our parents, huh?"

"I didn't *get it* from you," Quentin will say with calculated cruelty. "You forced it on me."

I'll be taken aback by that.

"Did you really think it was okay to just throw me into all that?" he'll ask me, his passion rising, passion I never saw in him before. "Not even a buffer or a condom or a… shield? Nothing?"

My brows will furrow. "I don't understand what you're saying."

"I know you probably thought raising me analog was gonna make me better or stronger or something, but… it didn't. It made me feel like a fucking freak."

I'll place my snifter down and say (sarcastically, I admit), "Well, forgive me for raising you the right way."

"Maybe you shouldn't have," Quentin will grumble. He'll throw his snifter at the grass, cognac flying everywhere. Then he'll fold his knees and wrap his arms around his legs, staring off into the night.

A bit of angry bile will sting my throat. "My parents were workaholics," I'll tell him. "By the time they retired, they didn't even know me. I didn't want that for you. I was home. I was there. I was present."

"I was the only one raised like that. Do you have any idea how awful it is not having what everyone else got to have?"

"I wasn't gonna let computers raise my son for me!" I'll say too loudly. "I was gonna be there for you! It wasn't just a principle thing to me. It was *personal*."

"Bullshit. You weren't there for me."

And I'll find myself glaring at my own son. "How the fuck can you say that?"

"Don't pretend. When Daddy got hurt, you chose him over me. I've been an afterthought ever since."

I'll rapidly blink at the absurdity. "You're not in a good mood."

"Did I not say I wanted to be alone?"

"What was that phone call about?"

Quentin will hesitate. "What does that have to do with anything?"

"It made you upset. What was that phone call about?"

"None of your fucking business."

"Oh, first I'm a bad dad for raising you *exactly* the way you've been telling the world they should've raised their kids, but now I'm a bad dad for trying to be there for you now. What's next, huh?"

"You can't just start because I said something."

"Your Daddy needed me. I knew a day like that would come eventually. That's the risk I took when I decided to marry a man thirty years my senior. That's what I agreed to take on, because you know what? He was worth it. And you know what else? *He's still here.* He still loves you. He still loves me. You have NO IDEA how lucky we are to have that!"

"You didn't even want to be a dad!" Quentin will blurt. "You didn't need me! Believe me, I know *perfectly well* how much you needed Daddy in your life. You wrote a whole fucking 800-page book about it. But you never needed me." And he'll look away, gripping his kneecaps tighter. "The only reason I'm suddenly worth anything to you is because I've been spouting your shit for the last year and a half."

And I'll frown, heartbroken, desperate to fix this. "I love you, Quentin," I'll whisper as earnestly as I can without breaking down myself. "I love you so much."

And Quentin will stay silent.

And I'll take a deep breath. "I don't know what more you want from me. I did the best I could."

"What good did that do?" Quentin will whimper. I'll be able to hear the tears in his voice. "It didn't make me better or special being 'above' everyone. Being the odd one out. No friends or anyone to talk to. Feeling like the world used to be so great before. Like I was stuck in a world of decay. No hope or optimism, just... disappointment." He'll shake his head. "I understand your reasons, of course I do, it's just..." And he'll get quiet for a bit. "You have no idea. No idea. It really fucked me up."

And I'll try not to cry hearing that. "When..." I'll stop, second guessing myself. I'll take another sip of cognac. "Right after *The Evening Show*, when Douglas Cameron tweeted all that stuff about you... He said on CNN you tried to kill yourself."

Quentin's eyes will soften.

But I'll refuse to believe it. "Was he lying?"

Quentin's chin will tremble. Tears will fill his eyes as he shakes his head.

"Oh God..." I'll whine, gripping Quentin as tight as I can.

And Quentin will gently pat my back, unconsciously suppressing his own grief, only to give into his emotions and hug me back.

And we'll stay there, hugging each other on the porch step, really sorry everything had to happen the way it did.

After twenty minutes of silence, when our bad feelings finally fade away, Quentin will retrieve the snifter he threw and bring it back to the step, helping me back to my feet. And we'll stay out there on the porch, peering in on Daddy and Phibs getting along so well in our absence. I'll look over at my son and notice a weight had been lifted off his shoulders. "So what was the phone call about?" I'll ask again, at long last.

That time he'll tell me. "I had an instinct about someone. Something he did. I didn't want it to be true, but... Turns out it was. Now I have to confront him about it. It's gonna ruin everything."

"That's all I get?"

"It's better you don't know."

I'll nod. "Why don't you want it to be true? Can you tell me that at least?"

Quentin will hesitate. "I've never told anyone this."

"Not even Phibs?"

Quentin will shake his head. "I think he suspects, but… Well, I really don't deserve him anyway."

"What do you mean?"

"When I…" Quentin will point to his gauged right ear, that sloppy hole-punch job. "I wasn't planning on it. It was right after Cameron was on CNN, calling me out with the truth. I was about to end the whole thing before he did that. Unplug. Everything. But then he did that, and I was so pissed off, so I kept blazing on, and… I think I'm in too deep now."

I'll furrow my brow, choosing to listen rather than say anything.

Quentin will look down at the empty glass in his hand. "And now this. It keeps getting worse, Zaddy. I really need to take a stand now, but… I don't know. I know Unplug can't keep going on like this, but if I say something, I just know I'm gonna lose something big. I can feel it. That's the problem. It needs to change, but I don't really want anything to really… change. If that makes sense."

I'll wait a moment before speaking. "What do you want to do?"

Quentin will shrug.

"Do you want to end it?" I'll ask.

Quentin will shake his head. "I want…" He'll look at me. "If Unplug was different than it is now… I mean *significantly* different… would you to still be proud of me?"

I'll frown, a realization dawning. "Is that what this is all about? Why you've been forcing yourself all this time?"

Quentin will hesitate, looking away.

I'll sigh. "It's your life, Quentin. Do whatever you want. But if you want me to be proud of you... just do it for the right reasons."

Quentin will give me a reassuring smile.

I'll place a hand on his shoulder and smile back, sliding the door open so we can rejoin our plus ones.

11.

schism

What will turn out to be the last biweekly Coalition meeting will occur the next day in its usual spot, the basement of Park Street Church. Jax will arrive first, surprised to see everyone else was late. And as he waits, he'll go over his pitch to Quentin for Munt's bail money, word-for-word, just as he practiced with Bro and Lossy the night before.

Esabell will arrive five minutes after the scheduled start time, shocked to see Jax there and nobody else. As she sits and waits, she'll go over her Festival pitch to Quentin, word-for-word, just as she practiced in her bedroom mirror the night before.

After ten minutes of Esabell and Jax soft-selling their individual hard sells to the Quentin in their minds, the real Quentin and Phibs will finally arrive. Phibs will be chipper as always, glad to see the band back together. That never seemed to happen anymore thanks to their chaotic schedules and workloads. But none of them had any idea what the unusually distracted Quentin planned to announce. The man himself will slowly grab a chair and join the circle, going over the accusation in his head, word-for-word, just as he practiced the night before.

"Okay, let's get started," Phibs will say, grabbing a pad and paper. "Who wants to go first?"

"I do!" Jax will blurt. That'll catch Esabell off guard.

"Just a minute," Quentin will murmur, still distracted. "I have something to say."

Jax, dependent on Quentin being in a good mood for his spiel to work, will relent.

Quentin will want to stand but his legs won't let him. "Jax?" he'll start, throwing away the formal introductory paragraph he originally wanted to say.

Jax will blink awkwardly. "Yeah?"

Quentin will hesitate. He'll pull a brass key from his pocket. Stand up. Walk over to the basement door. Slowly lock it.

Phibs will start getting concerned. Esabell too. Jax's mind will remain blank.

Quentin will pocket the key, sit down, and ask Jax, "Did you order Sprite McGinty to assassinate Ms. M?"

Esabell's blood will go cold, her bugged eyes darting over at Jax.

Jax will simply stare in shock. "Who?"

"I already know you did. I just want to hear you say it."

Jax's lips will start chapping with stage fright.

"Quentin," Phibs will say slowly, "what are you talking about?"

"When I first heard Sprite's monologue, I knew he didn't do it alone," Quentin will tell everyone. "So I made a call to D.C. PD and gave them an anonymous tip."

"You talked to the cops?" Jax will ask, appalled.

"I told them about you, Munt Bloom, Bro Williams and Lossy Berkowitz. Who you were. What you looked like. And I told them, should my information prove relevant in any way, that I wished to be informed." Quentin will pause. "Just last night I received a call that Munt Bloom had been arrested trying to break into D.C. Jail — the very same facility Sprite McGinty's awaiting trial in. Apparently, Munt climbed a wall, sawed his way in, ran left and hit a dead end. The guards caught him in seconds. They're calling in the stupidest prison break in history."

Jax will cross his arms and look away.

"Don't worry," Quentin will add. "He's not talking. They can't even prove he was going after Sprite. They just thought it was funny, considering what I told them. He's still in there, in a cell of his own, with a posted bail of $50,000." Quentin will throw in a smirk. "Which, I suppose, is what you wanted to talk to me about. Kinda wish I let you. I'd love to hear how you planned on selling it."

Jax won't know what to say to that.

Quentin will lean back in his chair. "So what was Munt doing, exactly? Was he trying to break Sprite out or Jack Ruby him? Cause both ideas really suck."

"Jax, is this true?" Esabell will ask.

Jax will shoot nasty eyes at Quentin. "No. It's bullshit."

"Really?" Quentin will say, amused. "Munt breaking into D.C. Jail, the same place Sprite McGinty's in… That's just a coincidence then?"

"Guess so."

"You know, I don't know which is more pathetic. The fact that you sent *Munt Bloom* of all people, knowing he knew you hired Sprite to blow up Natasha, or the fact that you actually had the chance to assassinate a woman with no security detail,

at 11 o'clock at night, on a Tuesday, and *failed*. Not that I condone killing anyone, but if you are gonna kill somebody, Jesus,
man, do it right! Get a gunman or a sniper or something. You
sent in a teenager with a stick of dynamite. What did you think
was gonna happen?"

"Munt's not gonna talk," Jax will counter. "He's locked in.
He's not some wishy-washy piece of shit like you."

Esabell will exchange scared looks with Phibs, who had
stopped transcribing long ago.

Quentin will stare back at Jax. "So it is true."

Jax will shake his head. "I can't believe I ever respected
you. You actually talked to the police? What the hell is wrong
with you?"

"Wait," Phibs will interrupt. "I'm confused."

"Why do you keep pretending we aren't at fucking
WAR?!" Jax will angrily ask Quentin. "You're right, I did have
a whole speech prepared to cater to your delicate feelings, but
why the fuck should I have? Why's it so fucking impossible to
get you to side with me on anything?!"

"Killing Natasha wouldn't have killed the bill," Quentin
will emphasize. "They're voting on it with or without her.
When they do, it's gonna pass. You know it will. So what then?
What's the next step of your master plan?"

Jax will shrug. "I guess I'll just have to burn Silicon Valley
to the ground."

"You're not serious?!" Esabell will exclaim.

"Of course I'm fucking serious!" Jax will snap back at her
with a furrowed brow. "They own everything! They own
everyone! They are a fucking cancer and we need to chemo
this bitch! If the Internet survives even a little bit, we failed!
You don't just sit around and *negotiate* with cancer! Yes, send-
ing in Sprite to kill Natasha was stupid. Yes, Munt getting

caught could've been prevented with a little more foresight. But you can't say in any way that I am not 100% committed to slaughtering every last fucking bit of the Hateful Eight." Jax will pause. "I said 'bit.' That's a pun. I love that I said that."

"You're a goddamn crazy person!" Quentin will cry out. "Everything you've done has only made it harder for anyone to be on our side!"

"Oh, big whoop, you don't get free advertising."

"What is it with you and that bill?" Esabell will ask. "It's such a non-issue! Don't you realize it means the Hateful Eight are actually caving to an Unplugged world?"

"Yeah, *on their terms!*" Jax will counter. "The bigger we get, the more money they make. Any 'caving' you think they're doing is just part of their master plan, featuring their usual MO, gaslighting and deception. Nothing's fucking changed."

Esabell will shake her head. "Well, anarchy's not a solution. If we want to win, we have to play the game by their rules."

"Tell me, what's actually being done to stop cyberbullying, huh?" Jax will ask her. "Why do you guys at the HCC only give a shit about the dead ones? What about the living, huh? Why do you think I am this way, Mother Theresa? That's something worth exploring. The *real* cyberbullied are the ones that refuse to negotiate with the terrorists that made their lives hell. But I suppose that doesn't mean shit to you. I didn't agree to the HCC for a fucking prayer circle and free marketing money. I wanted shit to stop, and you haven't done shit to stop any of it! So please, tell me how throwing thoughts and prayers at cancer is playing the game? Tell me."

Esabell will look away uncomfortably. "I wasn't talking about the HCC."

Quentin will look at Phibs, confused.

"I know this might not be the best time to bring it up, but…" Esabell will awkwardly look at Quentin, at Jax. "I've got a new idea. It's called the Unplugged Festival."

Jax and Quentin will instantly don expressions of disgust. "*What?!*" they'll cry in unison.

"I first thought of it after you hole-punched your ear," Esabell will say to Quentin. "It was such a dramatic, undocumented event. No cameras. No phones. Hundreds of people experiencing something in the moment. What if we did something like that on a larger scale? I'm talking a million people in the middle of nowhere. Live music. Movies. Drinks. Conversation. Sex. Drugs. Whatever. Nothing but life and fun, and not a single document or artifact that'll prove it even happened. Is that even possible nowadays? When was the last time that happened? Do you have any idea how amazing it would be if we could pull that off? It would be, like, the greatest achievement in human history!"

Jax will stare at her. "Are you fucking high?"

"The way I see it is… We've already got them on their fears. We've already got them on their guilt. So let's give them something to hope for. A little taste of the perfect Unplugged society. A concrete ideal for everyone to strive toward."

"Oh my God!" Quentin will groan, tightly gripping his hair. "Why do you keep fucking doing this?!"

Esabell will furrow her brow. "Doing what?"

"STOP MANIPULATING EVERYONE! God, it's every five seconds with you! What are you, an algorithm in human form?! Just stop it!"

Esabell will scoff, trying to hold back tears. "How fucking dare you."

"How fucking dare *YOU*!" Quentin will holler, his throat scratching. "A world without the Internet is not some fucking paradise! It's more fucking work! It's not a pharmaceutical commercial! It's not fucking orgasm!"

"I'm not saying it is!"

"Well, you're goddamn implying it is!"

"And why the fuck is it the 'Unplug*ged*' Festival?" Jax will add, feeling weird to be on Quentin's side on this.

Esabell will sit back, overwhelmed by the gang-up. "A lot of people call us that."

"Only because Roger Heffer tried to fuck over our hashtag in the early days."

"The data doesn't lie. A lot of people call us 'Unplugged.' We really need to embrace it."

"But that's not our name!"

"All I'm saying is maybe it should be." Esabell will wipe her flushed cheeks. "Cameron certainly didn't have a problem with that."

Quentin and Jax will gape in unison. "*Cameron*?!" Quentin will cry.

"*Douglas* Cameron?!" Jax will cry.

"The fuck you talking to him for?!"

"He's running for President, assholes!" Esabell will yell back. "He wants to sponsor the Festival! What did you want me to do, say no?"

"*He knows about the Festival?!*" Jax will shout.

"You told Cameron before telling us?!" Quentin will shout too.

"He called *me*, alright?" Esabell will counter. "He wanted to know what we had planned, so I told him my idea. At least he's actually giving it a chance!"

Jax will guffaw. "Oh, I definitely hate it now."

"Can we please get back to Jax? He's the one who tried to kill Ms. M!"

"I said no such thing."

"Why would you even consider doing *anything* with him?" Quentin will ask Esabell. "Don't you remember all that shit he tweeted about us?!"

"He tweeted shit about *you*," Esabell will say.

"He tweeted shit about ALL OF US! And, if you recall, he got me so upset that I ended up hole-punching my ear lobe in front of two thousand people, *which is what inspired the very thing he's sponsoring in the first place!*"

"If Cameron's the next President, we're IN! We got an ally in the White House! Unplugged will be immortalized!"

"STOP CALLING IT THAT!" Jax will screech. "It's 'Unplug,' you fucking bitch!

"I already told him we changed the name. We might as well start now."

"We're not doing the Festival!" Quentin will say with a laugh.

Esabell will gape. "Why the hell not?"

"Because we just forced the HCC on everybody."

"So?"

"*So*, you're forcing too much on everyone. Can't you just be happy with the progress we've already made?"

Esabell will scowl at Quentin. "You of all people telling me not to write my own algorithm."

Quentin will draw his brows together. "What?"

"'We have the power to kill them. We have the power to let them go. To undo everything.'"

"What are you saying right now?"

"That's YOU! YOU wrote that! I haven't contradicted the Manifesto ONCE with my methods! Not a single word!"

"Yeah, well…" Quentin's voice will fade out. "Maybe you should have. I dunno."

A heavy silence will fill the room, everyone suddenly aware of the loud ringing in their ears.

Esabell's lips will struggle to form words. "What?"

"Alright." Quentin will take a deep breath. "I shouldn't have…" He'll look at Phibs, that sad look on his face. "I-I-I shouldn't have—"

"Just say it already," Jax will whine.

Quentin will hesitate. "I wrote the Manifesto in a flash of anger. It's shitty writing. It's immature… and it's not how I feel anymore."

Esabell and Jax will look at each other, feeling weird to be on each other's side on this.

"Well, um…" Phibs will start, admittedly betrayed himself. "What do you feel now?"

Quentin will be moved by that teensy bit of support. "I think unplugging should be a way of life. Like being a vegetarian. People can do it together if they want, families, towns, but it needs to be their choice. There's no reason digital and unplugged people can't coexist. The all-or-nothing approach clearly isn't working, so I think we should all just dial it back a bit and just… be in the background. If it sticks, it sticks. At least we'll be happy in the meantime." Quentin will pause. "That's what I meant by us controlling our own algorithm. We've never had a say in the general zeitgeist before, but now we do. We don't have to destroy the greatest source of information in human history in the process."

Esabell will laugh bitterly. "You're calling *me* a hypocrite? You're the one sounding like Roger Heffer!"

"Don't pretend you wouldn't go on his show in a heartbeat to promote that Festival of yours."

Esabell will frown at that.

Quentin will look at Jax, at Phibs, back at Esabell. "If Unplug was really about the Internet, you'd all be agreeing with me on this. But it's not. Hasn't been for a long time."

"Of course it is," Jax will say.

"No." Quentin will shake his head slowly. "You're plunging the world into the Dark Ages to get back at your parents."

"Yeah, because they—"

"No. *Stop*." Quentin will close his eyes. "The only thing Millennials are guilty of is doing what everyone else was doing at the time, what they all thought was the right thing to do, because everyone said it was. If you were in their shoes back then, you would've done the same thing. They had no idea what damage they were causing. Of course they didn't. So why are we blaming them for it? Why aren't we blaming the Boomers? They're the ones that invented the damn thing!"

Jax will stare at Quentin with blank eyes. "See, this is what we get for putting an old-ass dude in charge."

Quentin will feel chills down his arms. "What?"

"Stop pretending you're one of us! You're not one of us!"

Quentin will gape a little. "I'm Gen A."

"You're practically thirty!"

"Still means I'm Gen A!"

"STILL MEANS YOU'RE THIRTY!" Jax will shout. "You can't speak for us!"

"Oh, all of a sudden?"

"Anyone siding with the Internet clearly does not have our best interest at heart!"

Quentin will scoff. "What do you think's gonna happen when it works? Do you really think you, Jax Halsteder, can survive in an Unplugged world? Your whole life has been computers and software. You don't know how to drive.

You've never planned a successful heist. What can you actually do, Nekoosa boy? What practical skills do you actually have that can *actually* be useful to the world?"

Jax's face will slack. He'll turn away.

Quentin will shake his head. "You have no idea. It is not easier, not by a long shot. It's scary. And lonely. And big. Nothing is made for you. It's just you and your own thoughts. You've never lived like that. Believe me, if *I* couldn't handle it… you won't even last a day."

Jax will frown, Quentin's words hitting him where it hurts.

Quentin will frown too. "I can't tell you how happy I've been, doing this. Having a voice. A following. I never understood why everyone was so addicted to social media, but now I think I do. And I haven't let it ruin me, which shows that it is possible to use both in moderation. In fact, it's actually quite natural." He'll look up at Esabell. Pull the basement key from his pocket. "Here." He'll toss it up to her. "It's yours now."

Esabell will catch the key. She'll stare it at lying on her palm, realizing Quentin's implication.

"You know my real manifesto now." Quentin will pause. "Follow it with just as much passion as you did the first one."

Esabell will clutch the key. Frown back at Quentin. "I'm not mellowing out just because you have."

Quentin will lower his eyes. Nod with sad acceptance.

Esabell will put on her coat. "If you guys wanna spend the rest of the night jerking off to the past, go right ahead. I only care about the future." She'll give Jax, Quentin and Phibs one last look. "Now if you'll excuse me, I've got a Woodstock to plan." She'll unlock the basement door and race upstairs.

Quentin won't move. Slumped in his chair. Eyes glued to the floor.

Jax will stand up, spit on Quentin's shoes, throw on his coat and march out, slamming the door behind him.

And it'll be just Quentin and Phibs in that room, that sad little room. "You're still here?" Quentin will murmur.

"Yup," Phibs will whisper back.

"Why?"

"Esabell's a liar with no self-awareness and Jax is a terrorist without a brain." Phibs will pause. "Guess I never really knew them, did I?"

Quentin will hesitate. "What about what I said?"

Phibs will give a halfhearted shrug. "It's what you want. Who am I to tell you otherwise?"

Quentin will smile a bit. "Thanks."

Phibs will smile back. "What are friends for?"

After two weeks of lawyer negotiations, the Unplug Coalition will officially dissolve. Quentin and Phibs will remain at their Emerson College headquarters under the official name '#Unplug,' relinquishing the postal Newsletter to Esabell on the condition that they get to keep its email equivalent. Jax will voluntarily relinquish his MIT headquarters to Esabell in exchange for $50,000, Munt Bloom's bail money, which Esabell will pay with donations from the Happy Child Campaign. Jax will then relocate his base of operations to Los Angeles, not too far from the YouTube Theater where the VMA Riots originally occurred.

On December 6, 2047, a letter will be issued to all official members of the Unplug Movement, formally announcing the schism and giving each member the option to align themselves with one of three distinct factions:

1. The Loyalists: believing in a literal interpretation of the Manifesto, prioritizing institutional policy and anti-cyberbullying activism above all else. Headed by Esabell Cortina-

Gomez, president of the Unplugged Movement and the Happy Child Campaign.

2. The Assimalists: believing in a peaceful coexistence between digital and non-digital living, customizable based on each member's preferences and comfort levels, with no political agendas, as per Quentin Wagner's original vision. Headed by Quentin Wagner, president of #Unplug, and Amphibian "Phibs" Cantell, vice president.

3. The Purists: believing extreme radical methods against the Hateful Eight as the only way to resist their control, prioritizing pure non-digital living by any means necessary. A decentralized collective run by Jax Halsteder, Munt Bloom, Bro Williams and Lossy Berkowitz.

The new membership numbers will be tallied in the days that follow. To everyone's shock (and disappointment), each faction will end up with roughly the same number of members, a near-perfect 33% split.

A further difference between the three camps will emerge in the last weeks of 2047: each faction will claim their leader was the one that committed the First Gauge on November 25, 2046. All Unpluggers' memories of the event will suddenly change, and yet somehow they'll be even clearer than they were before. Thousands of Assimalists will claim they saw Quentin gauge his own ears on a makeshift stage in Boston Common using a hydraulic hole-puncher. Thousands more Loyalists will swear with the same assurance that it was Esabell, not Quentin, that committed the First Gauge, and even more thousands of Purists will claim they saw Jax gauge his ears firsthand. It won't take a rocket scientist to see the impossibility of everyone telling the truth, not to mention only two thousand people were there that night, but no one will be able to prove anything since the First Gauge was never filmed or documented.

Despite the cataclysmic schism tearing Unplug apart, the rest of the world won't even notice. To them, the individual actions of the Loyalists, the Assimalists and the Purists will continue to be seen as the collective actions of the Unplugged Movement.

12.

labels

Esabell Cortina-Gomez, now in charge of the Unplugged Movement, the Happy Child Campaign, the postal Newsletter, the Northeastern headquarters, the MIT headquarters and an active roster of hundreds of thousands of Loyalists, not to mention the Unplugged Festival she promised Douglas Cameron, will suddenly find herself incredibly overwhelmed and exhausted. She'll spend weeks restructuring the organization, new hires left and right, understanding firsthand how nasty postage prices can be, how much of a nightmare it is to make a paper Newsletter week after week after week. Forced with no other choice, Esabell will announce at the start of the new year that a membership fee will now be required for members to receive an Unplugged Newsletter.

The new wave of income will be a great blessing at first, giving Esabell the freedom to do more, anything to get her more Newsletter subscribers so she can pay for the Festival. But every time Esabell will go to an HCC dinner or a networking conference, every time she'll make headlines for her charitable efforts, the ISP-controlled media will replay the VMA Riot footage, the Sprite McGinty tapes, the usual haunts. Growth will stagnate as quickly as it came, and Esabell will find herself trapped, privately wishing she hadn't thrown Quentin away so easily.

Jax, on the other hand, will be quite liberated by Quentin's absence. His army of Purists will don masks and take to the streets to protest Natasha's Bill before its House vote on March 13. They'll stand in the middle of traffic, intentionally jamming the drivers' autopilots, forcing them to drive around manually. They'll vandalize public spaces with graphic images of suicide, a sharp contrast to the mellow yearbook "before" pictures propped up by the Happy Child Campaign. They'll sabotage regional Wi-Fi networks during peak business hours. They'll arm themselves and rob e-commerce delivery trucks. They'll raid distribution warehouses to stop the flow of packages. They'll set electronic stores on fire, especially the ones that used to sell Internet-related products, products they already took off their shelves, all because they used to at some point in their history.

Police will have a hard time tracking the Purists down. Always losing them in crowds. Always unable to predict their movements. Their protests popping up all over the country with no discernable pattern, seemingly at random. Any hope of incrimination will be impossible due to their strict refusal to use the Internet, even in the name of helping their cause.

After yet another PR pivot gets squashed by the ISP-controlled media blasting footage of the Purists setting fire to yet another electronics store, Esabell will find herself at her wit's end. She'll call up Douglas Cameron and organize a meeting for February 20, 2048.

"I can't do it anymore," an exhausted Esabell will plead over an ice-cold Denver omelette. "No matter what I do, it's just... VMA this. Sprite McGinty that. Jax, Jax, Jax." She'll cover her face with a hand and let out dry, silent sobs.

Cameron will watch Esabell's vulnerable breakdown with secret delight. He'll give knowing eyes to his blonde bombshell of a Chaperone. "Capricorn, go on a smoke break, won't you darling?"

"Of course." Capricorn will gracefully stand and strut off.

Cameron will lean across the table and take Esabell's hand. "There, there."

Esabell will let out a relieved sigh. "I just want Unplugged to be big. I want the Festival to work. I can't fail this."

"I know." Cameron will pause. "How about this..." He'll sit back, releasing her hand. "I'm prepared to give the Happy Child Campaign a very generous donation. *Very* generous."

Esabell will smile and sigh, "Thank you."

"But I would like something in return."

"Just name it."

Cameron will finish what's left of his bellini. "What's your circulation?"

Esabell will blink, confused. "Of the Newsletter?"

Cameron will nod.

Esabell will have to think about that. "Almost a million. I have to double-check the exact—"

"That's alright. Do you have all their information?"

Esabell will stare. "Information?"

"You know, their names. Addresses. Phone numbers. Email."

Esabell will keep staring. "You want me to sell you their data?"

"My donation to the HCC has nothing to do with this conversation," Cameron will insist. "I'm just curious if you had them written down somewhere, that's all."

Esabell will swallow, conflicted. "Selling data is against the Unplugged Manifesto."

"But you didn't write the Manifesto, did you?"

"I'm still upholding it. I'm the only one upholding it."

"How's that working out for you?" Cameron will ask, throwing in a shrug.

Esabell will hesitate. "I can do it. It's just... the media—"

"They won't be a problem anymore." Cameron will smile. "They'll get off your back. They won't bring up the past anymore, the Purists, none of that. You'll be able to focus on the Festival, making it just as good as you want it to be."

Esabell will look into Cameron's friendly eyes, the ones giving her the wiggins. "That donation... It's not your money, is it?"

"It'll be an anonymous donation from a very generous benefactor."

"Whose money is it?"

Cameron will chuckle. "Do you really want to know? *Really?*"

Esabell will go quiet. She'll already know it's Digital Tomorrow, aka The Hateful Eight, aka the ones running the media crusade against her... aka the only thing stopping the Festival from happening on schedule. "Alright," she'll breathe. "I'll send over the addresses tonight."

Cameron will grin. "And everything else?"

Esabell will nod. "Everything else too."

An anonymous seven-figure donation will be given to the Happy Child Campaign the very next day.

Cal Vectors, practically a shut-in since he got fired from the Prudential Movie House, will turn on his TV that same day and instantly notice a new tone in the media's coverage of Unplugged. He'll hit shuffle and bounce around network to network, desperately looking for a single slander piece, but there'll be nothing. Overnight, the entire journalistic landscape had flipped in favor of Unplugged.

Cal will hop onto YouTube and find the VMA Riot footage inexplicably deleted. He'll search "Sprite McGinty" on Google and find zero results (not no results, *zero* results). He'll keep monitoring in the days that follow, but none of it will reemerge.

A couple weeks later, Cal will watch the newest episode of *Grey's Anatomy*, the storyline about an Unplugged patient and her "bigoted" parents culminating in tearful acceptance in favor of the Unplugger. And in a "very special episode" of his favorite sitcom, *What the Hyuk*, a painfully unfunny story will conclude with the conservative housewife character tearfully coming to terms with her "outdated" bias toward the movement, admitting she had been wrong about her teenage daughter, the Unplugger. And Hollywood celebrities will be making headlines for proudly siding with Unplugged — not the Happy Child Campaign, *Unplugged*, the ones rioting and stopping traffic and sabotaging and burning — signing petitions and speaking in PSAs to get others to join them. Cal will be so confused. He thought he was supposed to hate the Unpluggers. What the hell happened? What *changed?*

Cal will go back onto his computer and travel off the beaten path. He'll stumble upon a forum of anonymous freethinkers, former Unplugged allies the Movement had also shunned for daring to question their methods. They had all noticed the sudden change in coverage too. And Cal will start a conversation with one, finding himself a new friend. Instead of watching TV every day, he'll be on that forum every day, talking for hours and hours about Unplugged, how awful they are, how tired he is hearing about them all time, wishing everyone would just shut up about it.

Two days before the House votes on SETA, Jaymeigh Grady-Smith-Waterhouse-Price will receive an invitation to her friend Gezebelle's 25th birthday party the following evening. Ghiuliyette had also been invited, and she'll constantly pressure Jaymeigh to say yes. Jaymeigh will hesitate asking Natasha for the night off, worried how it would look if anyone found out Ms. M's Congressional Chaperone had gone to an Unplugger's birthday party the night before the big vote, let alone what drama might occur at the party once Gezebelle and her guests found out who Jaymeigh's boss was. But when she does ask Natasha, she'll be surprised to hear Ms. M allow her to go. Jaymeigh deserved a stress-free night off, especially after everything she did for her those past five months letting her boss stay in her apartment. Natasha knew fully well she could trust Jaymeigh to always do the right thing.

Unbeknownst to Natasha, Jaymeigh had been drifting deeper and deeper toward becoming an official member ever since the Unplugged Festival was announced. After all that Purist brouhaha following her and Natasha everywhere they went, extra security protocols making them nervous, three days of no stress or consequences in the beautiful fields of Vermont sounded like heaven to Jaymeigh. And no documentation of any kind would mean her boss would never find out. Problem was only official Unplugged members were allowed to attend, but Jaymeigh considered the price of a Newsletter subscription to be worth it considering all the good she'd be getting out of it.

Ghiuliyette will eagerly introduce Jaymeigh to all the Unpluggers at Gezebelle's party, assuring all of them that Jaymeigh was for real even if she wasn't an official member yet. Jaymeigh will find that all a bit strange, almost like Ghiuliyette was talking down a loaded gun in her face. And she'll start a conversation with Gezebelle the birthday girl, just casually, *hypothetically* asking her about the VMA Riots and Natasha's Bill and all the other intricate details about Unplugged. Gezebelle will be weirded out by all the invasive questions, not to mention how Jaymeigh kept accidentally calling it 'Unplug.' She would've assumed Jaymeigh to be some sort of narc had Ghiuliyette not vouched for her so enthusiastically. But she'll grin and answer all of Jaymeigh's stupid questions, that Loyalists don't riot, that no one's cared about Natasha since 2047, that the whole bill thing was a non-issue. Jaymeigh will be so relieved to hear it.

When it's time to exchange gifts, Jaymeigh will be excited for Gezebelle to open hers: a twenty-pack of Kodak disposable cameras. She had read a bit of Ghiuliyette's Unplugged Newsletter last December. The "How to Have an Unplugged Christmas" editorial had emphasized tinsel as the perfect symbolic Unplugged-approved decoration — which is why it had inexplicably sold in droves that year — and disposable cameras as the perfect gift for the Unplugger in your life. Their capacity of only 27 pictures perfectly represented an era of functional limitations and physical souvenirs. Having that little bit of insider Unplugged knowledge made Jaymeigh certain she'd be accepted as one of their own.

But Gezebelle will actually be quite offended by the gift. "I'm Pure, Jaymeigh! I don't believe in documentation!"

"I thought you were a Loyalist," Jaymeigh will say.

"Yeah, a Pure Loyalist!"

"But I thought Purists—"

"*Radicals,*" Ghiuliyette will correct her, embarrassed by the judging eyes on both of them.

Jaymeigh will hesitate. "I don't understand."

Ghiuliyette will immediately apologize to the group and roughly segregate Jaymeigh into the kitchen. "Look," she'll hiss, "there's Loyalists and Purists, right?"

Jaymeigh will nod. "And the Assimalists."

"No. Stop. Nobody cares about them." Ghiuliyette will harshly exhale. "Listen. There's Loyalists and Purists, right?"

"I guess."

"Okay. *Within* the Loyalists, there's the normal Loyalists, Analogs and Pures."

Jaymeigh's face will go numb. "Oh God."

"Normal Loyalists are okay with using electronics in Airplane Mode. Smartphones, tablets, digital cameras, MP3s, laptops, video games, you know. *Analogs* don't use electronics at all."

"Even though they're unnetworked?"

"Exactly. Polaroids, film cameras, microphones, acoustic guitars, vinyl, tape recorders, flip phones, they're all okay."

"But I got her disposable—"

"Gezebelle's a *Pure*. They don't believe in documentation. Just living in the present. No souvenirs, no videos, no photos, nothing."

Jaymeigh will scoff. "Why?"

"They believe documenting themselves now is just as bad as it was when we were plugged. To them, the only way to truly live in an analog world is by not falling back on the same addictive habits. Naturally they can't call themselves Pure without sounding like 'Purist,' so all Loyalists are supposed to call the Purists 'Radicals' to differentiate the two."

"Even normal Loyalists have to say that?"

"We have to be allies to our own. It's the only way we're gonna win."

"I thought Loyalists and Radicals were both Unplugged?"

"Loyalists are 'Unplugged.' Radicals are nothing."

"Against the Internet. You know what I mean."

Ghiuliyette will furrow her brow. "I don't understand."

"Forget it." Jaymeigh will scratch the top of her head. "What are you? Are you something?"

"Analog."

"Okay." Jaymeigh will look off. "I think." She'll turn around. Gezebelle will still be in tears, her friends trying to calm her down. "Does she know you're not Pure?" she'll ask Ghiuliyette."

"No!" Ghiuliyette will hiss. "Don't say anything."

"But you're both Loyalists."

"Pures hate Analogs. She'll never speak to me again."

"Why? Neither of you use electronics. Who cares what you do otherwise?"

"Because the Millennials were the ones that first brought back disposable cameras in the 20s, remember?"

"No."

"Well, they did. There was a whole thing about it in the Newsletter."

"So was the recommendation to buy disposable cameras in the first place!"

"That was December, Jaymeigh. This is March. If you really wanna be an official member, you *really* gotta keep up with everything."

Jaymeigh will sigh and return to the party and deeply apologize to Gezebelle for offending her. Afterwards she'll head home, say goodnight to Natasha and crawl into bed, determined never to become a member of the Unplugged, Festival be damned.

The next day, March 13, 2048, the House of Representatives will finally vote on the Stable Economic Transition Act. Natasha Mnozhynskyi will cast the first vote, a Yea, and return to her seat. For the next few hours, she'll watch a consecutive string of Democrats vote Yea, relieved after all those months pressuring them, greasing them, calling on favors, making promises she can only keep as Speaker.

When simple majority hits, applause will break out throughout the Chamber. Natasha will catch herself openly grinning. The rest of the session will be a formality, worthless vote after worthless vote, more Yeas with the occasional Nay, until it's time for Douglas Cameron's vote, the last one.

And he'll vote Nay.

A hush of surprised whispers will trickle throughout the room. The moment the session adjourns, Natasha will grab Jaymeigh and follow Cameron and Capricorn into the men's room. "What the hell was that?" she'll ask Cameron as he washes his hands.

Cameron will grin up at her reflection. "Natasha! The rumors about you are true, I see."

"Why'd you just vote against SETA?"

"Unpluggers vote."

Natasha will blink. "What?"

"I can't have documented support for Natasha's Bill thrown in my face at every primary debate. I'd never get the nomination."

Natasha will gape. "You son of a bitch."

"Oh, and about the whole Speaker thing…" Cameron will dry his hands. "You sponsoring SETA, fighting so hard to make it happen… I think it's made you too controversial a choice. I wouldn't get my hopes up if I were you."

Natasha will grab Cameron by the lapel and shove him against the wall. "You ASSHOLE! You fucking lied to me!"

"I have no idea what you're talking about!" Cameron will cry, feigning terror. "Jaymeigh dear, Capricorn, can you give us a moment?"

"NO!" Natasha will shout, pointing at Jaymeigh. "STAY HERE!"

Jaymeigh will remain where she is, disturbed. Capricorn will leave without hesitation.

Natasha will grit her teeth at Cameron. "You never turned them down, did you?"

"Who?"

"Digital Tomorrow. This was your plan all along. You knew I'd get SETA through the House if you promised me Speaker. That's what you told them. Now you get a fat check and clean hands at the same time."

Cameron will smile. "Natasha, you silly woman. Don't you know me by now? I don't do plans. I'm just a better im-proviser than you are."

Natasha will let Cameron go. "Do you have any idea what you've done?" she'll ask, her voice wavering. "What you made me do?"

Cameron will re-button his jacket with smug eyes. "You saved the economy from crashing and made some very pow-erful people *very* grateful."

"I almost got assassinated! My daughter won't even speak to me anymore! And I went against myself here! I always said Unplugged was the future! I was on their side from the beginning!"

Cameron will squint at that. "If you were *really* on their side, you would've voted Nay." He'll let himself out, leaving a distraught Natasha in the men's room with no one but her Chaperone to comfort her.

Support for the Unplugged Festival will reach dizzying heights in the weeks that follow, even after Cameron told Esabell to hit her members with a $200 Festival admission fee on top of their monthly subscription. The ISP-controlled media will publish Festival hype piece after Festival hype piece, conveniently leaving out all the breaking news of SETA passing in the Senate, STEA getting signed into law by President Myer, that horde of Purists taking to the streets of Silicon Valley to Molotov buildings, smash windows, attack cops, rubber bullets, tear gas, millions of dollars of property damage, hundreds of arrests and no one talking, blah blah blah, because why should they report all that serious *downer* stuff when the Unplugged Festival is right the corner! A monumental chapter in American history that hasn't even happened yet!

And finally, the Unplugged Festival will arrive. July 10th, 11th and 12th. Middle of nowhere Vermont, so vacant there won't even be a town close enough to give the location a name. No cameras. No reporters. Not even a written itinerary. Just a sea of memories from a million people. Some will be so high they can't even tell you if they wanted to. A whole lotta babies will be conceived that weekend, little Gen Cs. Even a baby being born on Night Two, can you believe it? No one will be able to believe the things said about that weekend. Elephants in Vermont? A sex pit where anyone could do anything to anyone who jumps in? A crazy man flying through the air with a guitar, playing a psychedelically intense guitar solo in the middle of "Start Me Up" by the Rolling Stones? Drugs, little pills, being handed out on trays like hors d'oeuvres? Everyone waking up on the second day singing "Let the Sunshine In" as loud as they can, clapping their hands over their heads in perfect time? An entire performance of *Hair* without a stage or lighting or any instrumentation of any kind, completely a cappella? Drinks every night? Buffets every morning? A freshwater lake of naked swimmers? Entire fields of people lying in trees, reading under trees, fucking against trees, lighting fire to trees, pissing all over trees? Explosions? Fireworks? The third day being just music, featuring thirty underground Unplugged artists, all of them playing classic hippie covers like Peter, Paul and Mary's "Day is Done" with modern lyrics from the POV of a cyberbullied kid who eventually unplugs? Or Neil Young's "Ohio" rewritten about Abcdé Meyer, Greggeriee James and Khaleesi Kaputchkin? Or an intentionally meta performance of Joni Mitchell's "Woodstock" with its original lyrics deliberately unchanged? Or a haunting performance of Barry McGuire's "Eve of Destruction," rewritten to describe the Internet era? Can any of it be believed?

And yet, that was the entire point. Everything could've happened. Nothing could've happened. It could all be true. It could've all been a waste of time, everyone covering their ass with a collective lie to justify them spending $200 on admission, months of Newsletter subscription fees and travel fare to Vermont. Because the only thing that mattered about the Unplugged Festival was that over a million people gathered together in one place, miles away from the closest cell tower or screen or camera or anything, and yet you could go there any other day and find just an empty field in Vermont. No evidence that anything even happened there at all. No secret cell phone hidden in someone's butthole. No secret drone flying over, taking pictures. No interorbital satellites seeking heat signatures. Nothing. If you weren't there, you missed it.

By Monday morning, no self-respecting American will ever be proud to say they're against the Unplugged Movement.

Throughout all this, ever since the schism, Quentin and Phibs will have tried their best to remain quiet and neutral, refusing to fall into corruption and manipulation the way Jax and Esabell did. As Assimalists, it was their job to keep rationality a top priority, to usher in critical thinking, to be a home for the burnouts, those Loyalist and Purist outcasts inevitably turned on for speaking the truth, for daring to questioning authority. But that won't happen. As a matter of fact, the exact opposite will happen.

As the Unplugged Festival gets closer and closer, the anger of the Purists getting hotter and hotter, the population of Assimalists will dwindle. The ones desperate to stay on the right side of history will join the Loyalists. The habitually cyberbullied, fed up by the inaction of the Happy Child Campaign, will grab a mask and join the Purists. Every week, Quentin and Phibs will count their numbers and realize they had less members than they had the week before, more and more deserters caving to societal peer pressure, until July 24, when Quentin and Phibs arrive late to their own meeting to find the conference room completely empty.

And then again on July 31, when Quentin and Phibs make sure to arrive extra early, only to have another hour of no-shows.

It'll happen again on August 7, another empty conference room. And Quentin will spend it the same way he had spent the last two, slumped in his chair, eyes empty and cold. Phibs will pretend, as he always had, that nothing was wrong. But Quentin will know it's over. He can take a hint.

"Alright," Quentin will rasp, standing up. "I'm calling it."

Phibs will check his watch. "It's been twenty minutes."

"No one's coming, Phibs."

"C'mon, we're late all the time. Just give 'em—"

"It's *over*." Quentin will stretch, his whole body aching. "I tried, but it's over." He'll plop back down in the chair with a frown he's never dared to show Phibs, the frown he always had growing up. "It's such a shame, you know?"

And they'll share a sad silence for ten uninterrupted minutes.

"I just want to thank you," Phibs will find himself murmuring. "You have no idea how much purpose you've given me."

"Is that what I'm gonna be known for?" Quentin will grumble. "That's my legacy? The guy that gave Phibs Cantell a purpose?"

"To me, absolutely. But to everyone else, you changed the world."

"I didn't do shit."

"Yes, you did! The only reason we turned off our phones in the first place was because of you. We got off our computers, gone out and lived. We went from a thousand little niche experiences to single culture. You united an entire generation. And you were right about everything. Sure, the Festival looks pretty sweet right now, but... one day people will ask why and how it happened and it'll all be traced back to you, that Manifesto you wrote. And when Jax goes too far —we all know he will — everyone will wish they were here in this room right now instead of out there with him."

"Stop."

"And when people see the big picture, the before, middle and after of Unplug, they'll see you were the only one with brains. The only one with critical thinking. All those children out there, ruining your vision with emotion and impatience, they were all wrong and you were right. They'll know you were the one, *the only one,* who did the First Gauge that night. They'll know the Happy Child Campaign was nothing more than a manipulative reaction to D.U.M.P, that it routinely committed donation fraud. That Unplug was never about violence. That the Manifesto was not the way what you wanted it to be. That you stuck to your guns, even when no one else showed up, because you believed in the truth when everyone was more interested in lies—"

"I can see it now," Quentin will interrupt. "Our parents were so obsessed with repeating history, creating something of their own by taking just as much from their parents. They're the ones that taught us to hate everything as-is, everything that wasn't our own making. That it's okay to cherry-pick what parts of the world to keep and what parts to rip away. We're not the opposite of the Millennials, we *are* the Millennials." He'll go quiet for a bit. "We're all just like them."

Phibs will start getting nervous. "You're nothing like them. You're better than them. They did nothing to stop the Internet from getting this bad. You did. You can't compare yourself to the rest of them."

"That's the thing, what did I actually change? There's still mental health abuse. The Hateful Eight's still around, sticking their grubby little fingers into everything, manipulating everyone for profit. People are still being bullied into conforming. The media's still biased. The truth's still hidden behind a paywall. Nothing's actually changed. It all just moved around a little bit." Quentin will close his eyes. "Killing the Internet won't make the world a better place."

"Yes, it will."

"No," Quentin will whisper, his energy spent. "When Unplug becomes the establishment, a whole new generation will revolt against it. They'll spend their whole lives hating us for what we did. Hating *me* for what I did. For taking it away from them." Quentin will stand. "And why? I'm not happier. I'm not popular. I'm not proud of myself. I'm not stronger. I'm nothing."

Phibs will look up at Quentin, on the verge of tears himself.

Quentin will look away. Take a deep breath. Walk to the door.

"Call me tomorrow," Phibs will speak up.

"Go home, Amphibian."

"Promise me you'll call tomorrow."

"I said go home—"

"OKAY!" Phibs will shout, unable to hold it in anymore. "I WILL, ALRIGHT?!"

Quentin will stop at the door and look back, his heart breaking at the sight of a teary-eyed Phibs.

Phibs will remove his glasses to wipe his wet eyes, his cheeks getting all pink. "But you gotta call me tomorrow, okay?"

Quentin will stare.

"Promise me," Phibs will insist.

Quentin will nod. "Okay."

"Promise me you'll call."

"Okay."

"No, *promise me*. Promise me you'll call tomorrow. Say 'I promise I'll call, Phibs.'"

Quentin will nod with more assurance. "I promise I'll call, Phibs."

Phibs will wipe his face a bit more and put his glasses back on. "Good. You promised."

"I promised."

Phibs will point. "You promised you'd call."

Quentin will nod once more and walk away without a word.

That night, Quentin will drive out to that old Worcester apartment of his. He'll unlock the door. Let himself in. Turn on his old laptop, the one he wrote the Manifesto on. He'll hop onto one of those random livestream sites and create an account. He'll start broadcasting out to the world, his face lit only by the screen itself. A few people will chime in to the stream, watching Quentin just sitting there. All he'll be able to see of them is their location, little green dots on a map. India by the looks of it. They're not going away. They're curious to see what he does.

And Quentin will smile, imaging those Indians so many miles away. It's like they're practically sitting with him in that shitty little apartment of his. "My father told me a story once," he'll tell that mysterious audience of his, now over a hundred. "When he was sixteen, the one thing he wanted most in the world was a pocketwatch. Everyone in the world wore wristwatches back then. He hated them. They were so boring, he said. Everyone that had one was boring. He didn't want to be like them. He wanted a *pocketwatch*. He wanted to be able to pull it out, click it open, look at the time, make a little hum about it, click it shut and put it away. He said people always looked so cool when they did that in movies. He wanted that to be his thing. Of course he didn't want the pocketwatch so much as he wanted to live in that world, but still. That was the best he could do. So be it. Why not? But everywhere he went, gift shops, antique stores, the only pocketwatches he could find were those cheap, shitty novelty ones. Nothing like the real thing. The real ones were expensive in their day. Artistically designed. Personalized. They weren't made of plastic-coated steel from Bangladesh. They didn't break if you dropped it once. They didn't die on their own after two weeks. It was a real part of a person. An extension of themself. Worth being in their motherfucking pocket. Truth is, he was wasting his time looking for a pocketwatch like that. They really didn't make them like that anymore. Even the ones in the movies were just cheap props. So he moved on. One day, years later, when he was at Emerson, he was sitting in a common room, looking around at the other students. And he noticed they kept checking their phones for the time. They'd pull them out, click the button, look at the time, make a little noise, click it off, and put it back in their pocket. That's when he realized... he was there. He was finally in that world he wanted to be in so badly. And those phones were expensive too. Designed by engineers. Made out of NASA-grade materials. Personalized. Worth being in your motherfucking pocket." And Quentin will nod at that. "At that moment, you know what he wanted more than anything?"

A moment of silence. Over two hundred viewers now, almost three.

"A wristwatch," Quentin will whisper. He'll think on that a little bit more. The irony of it all. Then he'll make eye contact with the camera, all three hundred pairs of eyes looking back through the same lens. "This is so much better than the last time. I'm glad something good came out of it at least."

Another bit of silence. Stillness.

Quentin will reach for his semi-automatic pistol, the one he bought so long ago. He'll open the chamber to see if it's loaded this time. Yup.

Just then, a little blue dot will pop up, a thumb's up bubble floating up the length of the screen. After a bit of confusion, Quentin will realize what it was: a reaction from a member of his silent audience. An actual human interaction. And he'll smile. "Oh yeah," he'll murmur. "Definitely worth it."

And without giving himself a moment to change his mind, that beautiful mind of his, my beautiful baby boy, my son…

13.

conspiracy

Douglas Cameron will instantly be made Democratic frontrunner thanks to his *12 Angry Men* vote of Nay against SETA, and the ISP-controlled media will report at length how hard he tried to fight and kill that horrible bill before it ever made its way to the House floor.

Fresh off her massively successful Unplugged Festival, Esabell Cortina-Gomez will be personally by the Cameron campaign invited to give a speech on Night Two of the DNC. Taking the podium, Esabell will publicly thank Douglas Cameron for his valiant support of the Unplugged Movement, making sure to mention his very generous, selfless donations to the Happy Child Campaign.

On the last night of the DNC, Douglas Cameron will take the stage to accept the Democratic nomination and make a promise that will catch the world by storm: "When I'm President of the United States, my first act will be the establishment of Non-Digital Cities. No Wi-Fi. No Bluetooth. No network of any kind. No cell towers. No social media. No self-driving cars. No invasive screens. No digital hindrances. Every small business. Every downtown district. Every school.

Every home. At every level, all the way up to city government. I promise, it will be the highest priority of my administration to have fifty Non-Digital Cities up and running by 2050, starting with my native San Francisco."

The Convention will erupt in applause.

"A Non-Digital City is the best environment for American prosperity," Cameron will continue. "It will mean more jobs. It will mean more revenue. It will mean safer streets. It will mean safer schools. It will mean happier people everywhere."

Through the Purists' sabotage efforts of Cameron campaign centers, Munt Bloom will get his hands on a classified plan, an insider document that actually defines what a Non-Digital City is. A key factor will be a 500% increase in the average price of goods and services, no doubt a kickback for Cameron's friends at Digital Tomorrow. A true Loyalist would have no problem paying extra to live in a Non-Digital City — or at least Cameron's puppet Esabell can use her Newsletter to bully them into not having a problem, lest they be exiled from the city.

Reading the stolen documents will actually make Jax sick. It's already bad enough there are ads now on every letter, every package, constant reminders that the Hateful Eight are getting richer than ever before. They have to take over entire cities too?

With the help of Munt, Bro and Lossy, a masked Jax will record a video, his voice distorted, openly condemning Douglas Cameron, accusing him of secretly hijacking the Unplugged Movement, revealing the secret agenda behind his Non-Digital Cities, and concluding with an ominous vow of a large-scale act of retaliation against the Hateful Eight.

The Purists will send Jax's tape to a single LA news station and the entire faction will go dark. It'll take a few days for the world to notice, but one day someone will: no more masked men. No more Wi-Fi outages. No more street protests. No more vandalism. No more e-commerce trucks getting hijacked. No more warehouses overrun. No more electronic stores on fire. Nothing. Complete radio silence.

Meanwhile, Cameron's PR team will ask Esabell if she could allow them to curate the Newsletter for her. Esabell will say yes, thankful for one less thing to worry about. The new management will then shift the Newsletter's tone away from irrelevant World news and mixed-messaged point/counter-point pieces and instead only focus on general Liberal talking points: civil rights, social programs, minority representation, intersectionality, affordable health care, etc. Most of the time the stories in the Newsletter won't have anything to do with the Unplugged Movement, except for the occasional op-ed from Esabell — credited to her, at least — reminding everyone that a vote for Merv Yarrow (the Republican candidate, Cameron's opponent) or any Third-Party candidate would be a vote for a future where Unplugged has been made illegal, everything great about analog living taken away *forever*, and that a vote for Cameron is the only way to guarantee that future won't happen.

On August 20, 2048, Cal Vectors will log onto his favorite Anti-Unplugged forum and discover a pinned message, a vague announcement from the moderator that the forum has gotten too big, law enforcement might be monitoring their discourse, telling everyone to text their ZIP code to a specific phone number to receive info on the closest in-person Anti-Unplugged meetings near them.

Cal will text the number and get an automated message back with three addresses, one in Austin, one in Houston and one in Dallas, as well as the dates and times for each location's meetings. Luckily for him, the next meeting at the Austin location will be that night at 7.

Cal will approach the gymnasium with an odd feeling in his stomach. He hadn't been out of the house for over a year, let alone in the company of other people. A part of him will feel like it's a trap. But he'll see another man awkwardly walk in, giving Cal a knowing nod as he held the door open for him, and Cal will suddenly remember how great it was to be in a room full of believers again.

That meeting will be a godsend to Cal. Over a hundred people from all walks of life, rich, poor, fat, short, young, old — all of them guys — will spend two hours verbalizing what they all already know to be true: the Unplugged Movement should never have happened. Anecdotes will flow out like water, each bearing a similar theme, how "illegal" it feels now to be on the Internet, or to even verbally disagree with the almighty Unplugged. Stories of workplace drama, firings, divorces, assaults, all centered around someone daring to speak the truth out in public. There'll be sad moments too, like a biker named Cletus moving himself to tears as he describes how openly discriminated he's been just for having gauged ears, ears he had stretched decades ago. And when no one else seems to have the courage to follow such a harrowing tale, Cal will give his, how his dream job of twenty-five years was taken away from him because he refused to gauge his ears out of mandatory solidarity. The room will applaud with genuine sympathy, and Cal will feel seen, so much more than he did when he was just online.

After the Austin meeting, Cal will find himself itching for another one, so he'll get in his car and drive all the way up to Dallas to catch a meeting there, and then he'll drive to Houston for the meeting they were having the night after that, and then up to Oklahoma City for the one the night after that, and then back to Dallas, then back to Austin, then back to Oklahoma City again before going back to Hoston, and so on, just so he'd have an Anti-Unplugged meeting every night of the week, every one filled with likeminded men, brave patriots, going off on Unplugged and how it ruined their lives.

Cal will lay awake in whatever seedy motel room he had booked for the night and replay all the stories in his travels that really stuck out to him. Like that old widower in Oklahoma City who couldn't video call his grandkids anymore. That cooking influencer in Houston who never needed to be in front of the camera, suddenly forced to sell his brand in-person with a non-photogenic face, suffering the commercial consequences. That handsome bodybuilder in Dallas who had always depended on dating apps for sex because of his abysmal lack of social graces, unable to maintain a conversation with someone or even approach a girl at a bar. That middle-aged Austin man who finally caved and got a social media account after decades of ridicule for not having one, only to face more ridicule for being on social media at all, contributing to the machine killing kids. Above all, Cal had heard the same comment in every city, every night, always from a different man: the media was now in the hands of the Unplugged, at best conveniently leaving out the occasional vandalism, at worst covering up the gruesome Silicon Valley Riots, all in the name of their sinister agenda, whatever it that may be.

On Friday, September 18, 2048, after a long day at the office, Natasha will surprise Jaymeigh with a little thank you gift, two tickets to a theatrical adaptation of Dostoevsky's *Crime and Punishment* at the Kennedy Center that evening. Jaymeigh will be downright giddy with excitement, begging Natasha to go with her, but Natasha will humbly refuse, insisting she take a nice three-hour break away from her. And so Jaymeigh will give the second ticket to Ghiuliyette, their mutual love for Dostoevsky being the only thing keeping their friendship alive after Gezebelle's disastrous birthday party.

Jaymeigh will meet Ghiuliyette outside the Kennedy Center, still in her work clothes, her laptop bag strapped over her shoulder, and she'll suddenly remember how fiercely an Analog Ghiuliyette was. What if the sight of her work laptop gets Ghiuliyette all triggered, ruining the night for both of them? And so Jaymeigh will make an excuse to return to her car and discreetly fish the official Department of Congressional Chaperones laptop out of her bag... only to find two Dostoevsky novels in the place where the laptop normally resided, *Demons* and *The Idiot*. And she'll recognize those copies. Those were the ones she gave Natasha months ago for her birthday, the ones she always kept on her desk...

A cold chill will spike down Jaymeigh's spine. She'll hop into the driver's seat. Speed out of the parking lot. Zoom down Independence Avenue as fast as she can. When she gets to the Rayburn, she'll practically skip the security checkpoint, security forcing her to double back and scan her ID. Then she'll race hard to the elevators, catching one just before it closed. Up five floors she'll go, and around the corner she'll see a light coming from Natasha's office.

Jaymeigh will burst in. The first thing she'll see is Natasha's shocked, terrified, obviously guilty face. Then, and only then, will Jaymeigh notice the ten others in the room, members of their IT department, their computers plugged into Jaymeigh's laptop opened wide on Natasha's desk. And Jaymeigh will recognize the frozen face on one of their screens: a dimly lit Quentin Wagner, a home video open in what appeared to be a deepfake generator. On another screen, Jaymeigh will recognize her official Department of Congressional Chaperones watermark open in Photoshop. A man with a neckbeard was still typing, his screen closest to Jaymeigh. It was an email from Jaymeigh to Natasha, one he was writing on the spot.

It won't take long for Jaymeigh to piece together what Natasha was doing. She'll give Natasha one last knowing look before turning away. She'll hear her boss tripping on the IT men as she raced out of the office. "Wait!" Natasha will cry. "Jaymeigh! Please!"

"Get away from me!" Jaymeigh will smack the elevator down button.

"Let me explain!"

"I DON'T WANT TO KNOW!"

Natasha will stand there, her heart breaking. "Please."

"I don't care." Jaymeigh will shake her head, refusing to look at Natasha. "I can't do this anymore. I can't. I'm sorry."

"*No*, I really need you to understand."

"Iverna was right about you."

"No!"

"Fine!" Jaymeigh will say with a bitter laugh, finally turning to face Natasha. "Go ahead! Tell me everything! Then I'll go tell Sharon at the DCC and you'll be finished! Go ahead! Please! Put me in that position!"

Natasha will stare, horrified.

"WELL?!" Jaymeigh will click the elevator button some more. "You've got twenty seconds. C'mon. Tell me something. Anything. Do that to me."

Natasha will swallow. "Cameron can't be President."

"He's a Democrat."

"You've seen what I've been through. You've seen what that fucker did to me. He's a fucking pig."

"He's a *Democrat!* He's your fucking party! What, just because you can't control him you'd rather give the country away to Yarrow the Fascist?!"

"Jaymeigh," Natasha will say gently. "You know me."

"No, I don't think I do." Jaymeigh will glare into Natasha's eyes. "Nothing makes sense anymore. You're nothing like I thought you were. You're not what Iverna thinks you are. You're not what Unplugged thinks you are. You're not what Cameron thinks you are. You're not even who *you* think you are."

Natasha will frown. "Then what am I?"

Jaymeigh's breath with quicken. The elevator will ding, both doors opening.

"C'mon!" Natasha will shout at her. "C'mon, Chaperone! Tell me what I am!"

Jaymeigh will watch the elevator doors close themselves, unable to move. "I think…"

Natasha will inhale sharply, waiting, worrying.

Jaymeigh's whole body will tremble. "I think I'm too impartial for politics." She'll turn around and burst into the staircase, racing down to her car. She'll flake on Ghiuliyette. She'll miss the show. She'll go home and cry instead.

The next day, Jaymeigh Grady-Smith-Waterhouse-Price will officially resign from the Department of Congressional Chaperones. She won't give a reason why. She won't report what Natasha was doing. She'll never speak what happened to anyone.

Natasha with be reassigned to a far younger, far stupider Chaperone named Tricksey, and she'll fight through her the of betraying Jaymeigh by doubling down on her plan to screw Cameron out of the White House. Using her former Chaperone's laptop and official watermark, she'll send herself a series of fake emails — automatically authenticating them in the process — and then leak those fake emails to the gullible hands of the Anti-Unplugged network sprouting up all over the country. The emails, if compiled and placed in chronological order, will make no sense whatsoever, each one contradicting the one before it, failing to paint a cohesive narrative. But no one will go through the effort of doing that. Individually, each email will be enough to get the ball rolling.

Cal Vectors will first hear a Douglas Cameron conspiracy theory on October 2, 2048 during one of his nightly meetings, having no idea like everyone else that it was made up single-handedly by Natasha Mnozhynskyi. There's no way it couldn't be true. Of course Douglas Cameron was a Purist plant that successfully infiltrated the U.S. government, intent on creating totalitarian analog cities to strip America of its rights and eventually abolish the Constitution. He'll hear another theory in another city's meeting, and then another one in another city, over and over, and it'll all add up. Of course Douglas Cameron was a member of the Illuminati, and Antifa, *and* that Satanic cannibalistic child sex trafficking cabal those QAnons are still go on about. Q had posted all his accusations online, right? So of course that's why Cameron wanted to be President. It's the only way he could make the Internet illegal and keep Q silent about his devilish affiliations.

Cal will learn the worst revelation of them all on October 13. Quentin Wagner himself got really close to exposing Douglas Cameron for who he really is, apparently, and for that Cameron had him killed and staged his murder to look like a suicide. Cal will watch a video — officially watermarked by the DCC no less — of Quentin telling the camera about the real Douglas Cameron, all his wicked plans for those who oppose him, how important it was for everyone to vote for Merv Yarrow, Douglas Cameron's greatest enemy, the man determined to put the monster in jail. And Cal will cry at the sight of the gun pointing at Quentin's head, his unseen assassin just off-screen, before it shoots him.

Cal will watch the same video five times over seven days, every rewatch driving Quentin's words deeper and deeper into his brain. He won't be able to watch it a sixth time all the way through. Not because he didn't want to, but because the meeting in Dallas got cut short thanks to a police raid, Cal and the three hundred other patriots arrested and charged with conspiracy and being in possession of classified documents. Apparently that handsome bodybuilder who couldn't get laid was an undercover cop. One of Cameron's cronies, no doubt. Had to be. Which meant it was all true. All of it. There was no other explanation.

Stuck in a Dallas jail cell, Cal will be left with no other option but to call his brother to bail him out. Three hours later, Jim Vectors will walk into the cell block with a cruel look of disappointment on his face. "How could you believe all that shit?"

"It's not shit," Cal will whisper, patting Jim down to see if he's wearing a wire. "It's all true. Cameron had Quentin Wagner killed."

"Don't be ridiculous."

"I saw the footage, Jim! I fucking saw it, alright?"

"That video's been debunked, Cal. None of it was real."

"Says who? Snopes? The media? You're gonna believe the fucking *media* over your own brother?"

"You're losing your mind."

"Cameron owns Unplugged now! He's trying to control our minds! He wants us off the Internet to keep us quiet about what he's planning—"

"Oh yeah? What's he planning?"

Cal will gape, hesitating. "Probably something really fucking bad."

"So, nothing."

"DON'T BELIEVE IT!" Cal will cry, pointing at him with bugged eyes. "None of it! It's all a fucking lie, Jim! Cameron tweeted against Unplugged two years ago, before the Boycott. Now he's all for it? No-no! This goes way back. It was all part of the plan. Keep everyone distracted while his cogs were in motion. And now it's huge because no one even stopped to think *why*, why would Cameron have a problem with 'just a little boycott?' But it wasn't just a little boycott, now was it? It was all him! The Boycott was all him! It was all part of his plan all along!"

Jim will rub the bridge of his nose. "Don't you think it's more likely that Cameron was just being a two-faced politician, flipping for votes?"

"No, no way. Think about it. There's no way that many people would ever get off the Internet that fast. Not voluntarily. Not in such a short length of time. I'm telling you, Jim, they're all in on it. All of 'em. They're planning something, I'm telling you. They're fucking burning down cities so Cameron can build them back in his own image and the media's covering the whole thing up for them!"

Jim will close his eyes. "Jesus Christ."

"What do you think they were doing up there in Vermont, huh? Over a million people and not a single photo? Not a single video? That doesn't seem *suspicious* to you?"

"That was the whole point!"

"SAYS WHO?!" Cal will shout. "Cameron?! Oh, I bet he did! What were they really doing up there, Jim? Where did they really go?! What are they planning?!"

"Don't you hear yourself? The fuck happened to you, Cal? You were the guy at Thanksgiving complaining about everyone shitting on movie theaters without ever going in!"

"STOP BELIEVING EVERYTHING YOU SEE!" Cal will shout. "Do your own research, Jim! Stop being a fucking idiot! Ask anyone! Everyone knows what's really going on! Everyone's talking about it!"

"*Everyone?* Cal, when was the last time you even talked to an Unplugger? When was the last time you were in a room with someone that wasn't a complete nutcase?!"

"You're the nutcase, Jim. They're all fucking liars. Every Unplugger's a fucking liar."

"No, they're not! Gabe and Flora unplugged months ago. Their whole brand's offline now, and they're *thriving!* They actually love what they do now. They've been asking us for weeks how to find you."

"Why?!" Cal will ask, suddenly scared.

"So they can apologize!" Jim will scoff at Cal's paranoid demeanor. "Cal, you were right about Unplugged. We all shoulda listened to you back then. But just because you were right about that doesn't mean you're right about this!"

Cal will shake his head with wide eyes. "You better not have fucking told them where I am."

"You're not listening to me."

"You told them I'm here, didn't you?"

"Cal—"

"Fuck no. I'm not going with you. Fuck off."

Jim will sigh. "Cal, I've already paid your bail. You can't stay here."

"FUCK OFF!" Cal will scream. He'll cross his arms and face the cell wall.

Jim will frown, too overwhelmed to argue. He'll return to his car and wait for Cal to stumble out so he can drive his brother home. But hour after hour, the sun coming up, Jim will wait with no sight of Cal. He'll reluctantly start the engine, put it in drive and drive back to Austin alone.

14.

terrorists

Natasha Mnozhynskyi will get a bit too desperate in her lust for revenge those last few weeks before Election Day, throwing out a few Hail Mary theories to the Anti-Unplugged about how stupid Douglas Cameron is, that he's nothing but a weak puppet for, I dunno, North Korea. Yeah, he's evil AND stupid, a nasty combination that totally doesn't contradict each other and would absolutely *suck* to have as President!

But alas, it won't be enough. On Election Day 2048, millions of people will cast their vote, having already made up their mind months ago, entirely unswayed by Esabell's fearmongering and Natasha's conspiracy nonsense, and that choice is Douglas Cameron, winner of 49% of the popular vote and a mere 273 Electoral Votes.

Esabell will scream, actually scream, so happy that Unplugged is now a legitimate political movement associated with a motherfucking President. Cameron will raise a private toast to her, thanking her for all her help, emphasizing how eager he is to start their next project together, converting San

Francisco the overpriced digitally plagued city to an even more overpriced analog utopia.

Of course no one will see 11/11 coming. No one will have answers on 11/12. In fact, it'll take fifteen years for the 11/11 Commission to piece together exactly what happened that day and why, complete with a minute-by-minute timeline of the planning, execution, all the moving parts. In the meantime, however, the world will tell itself stories to fill that void, horrible myths, legends, just to try and make sense of it all, but to no avail. One thing just cannot be understood: how did a twenty-two-year-old MIT dropout from Nekoosa, Wisconsin pull off the greatest act of global terrorism in history?

Here's how.

The Internet, a wireless marvel of human ingenuity, is in actuality a very physical being, hundreds of thousands of miles of cables connecting all the continents, running under the sea and popping up on beaches, a grand total of 187 physical networks connected by 805 individual cables that are all supposed to be buried deep in the sand, often popping up from natural erosion. And because the Internet belongs to no single nation, the locations of all 805 cables are required by law to be public knowledge.

There are 98 cables in the United States alone, the state with the most being Alaska with 24. The other 74 can be found on various beaches in California, Florida, Hawaii, Massachusetts, New Jersey, New York, Oregon, Rhode Island and Washington State, as well as Puerto Rico, the U.S. Virgin Islands, American Samoa and Guam. The remaining 707 cables can be found on the coasts of Algeria, Angola, Antigua and Barbuda, Argentina, Aruba, Australia, the Bahamas, Bahrain, Bangladesh, Barbados, Belgium, Belize, Benin, Bermuda, Brazil, Brunei, Bulgaria, Cameroon, Canada, Cape Verde, the

Cayman Islands, Chile, China, Colombia, Comoros, the Congo, Costa Rica, Côte d'Ivoire, Curaçao, Cyprus, the Democratic Republic of the Congo, Denmark, Djibouti, Dominica, the Dominican Republic, Ecuador, Egypt, Equatorial Guinea, Estonia, the Faeroe Islands, the Federated States of Micronesia, Fiji, Finland, French Guiana, French Polynesia, Gabon, Germany, Georgia, Gibraltar, Ghana, Greece, Greenland, Grenada, Guadeloupe, Guatemala, Guernsey, Guyana, Haiti, Honduras, Hong Kong, Iceland, Indonesia, India, Iraq, Iran, Ireland, Israel, Italy, Jamaica, Japan, Jersey, Jordan, Kenya, Kuwait, Latvia, Lebanon, Libya, Lithuania, Madagascar, Malaysia, the Maldives, Malta, the Marshall Islands, Martinique, Mauritius, Mayotte, Mexico, Monaco, Morocco, Mozambique, Myanmar, Namibia, the Netherlands, New Caledonia, New Zealand, Nicaragua, Nigeria, Norway, Oman, Pakistan, Panama, Papua New Guinea, Peru, the Philippines, Poland, Portugal, Qatar, Réunion, Romania, Russia, Saint Lucia, Saint Kitts and Nevis, Saint Vincent and the Grenadines, Samoa, Saudi Arabia, Senegal, Singapore, Sint Maarten, South Africa, South Korea, Spain, Sri Lanka, Sudan, Suriname, Sweden, Syria, Taiwan, Tanzania, Thailand, Togo, Trinidad and Tobago, Tunisia, Turkey, Turks and Caicos, Ukraine, the United Arab Emirates, the United Kingdom, Uruguay, Venezuela, Vietnam and Yemen.

And they can be cut with an ax.

Normally the cables within each network are wired to back each other up in the case of severance, but if all 805 cables were to be cut at the exact same time, the Internet will be landlocked, broken up into a handful of tiny Internets limited by borders and gaping oceans.

At 8:00 AM GMT on November 11, 2048, the first phase of the attack, made up of 1,610 Purist volunteers, two men per cable with an ax between them, will find their way to their assigned destinations, knowing how crucial their precision is to the integrity of the entire operation. The moment 8:00 AM strikes, they will strike, having only two minutes to sever the cord lying at their feet, and the moment they does, the shit will hit the fan for everyone else.

Phase One will succeed with ten seconds to spare. At 8:02 AM, the global economy will crash instantaneously, the whole world suddenly aware that some really bad shit's going down.

The second phase of the attack, made up of 10,000 men, will be against the root servers. Root servers are responsible for decoding domain names into their corresponding IPs. Without them, all web addresses would be reduced to incomprehensible code numbers, making web surfing nearly impossible unless the user knew their destination's exact IP address by heart.

There are 13 root servers in the world, each given a letter and backed up to redundancy across a total of 1,497 sites, and just like the locations of the beach cables, the street addresses of the root servers are legally required to be public available. The sites themselves look no different than simple office complexes, except for the extremely armed security, that is.

The second wave of Purists will start their assault on the root servers at 8:03 AM, having only 27 minutes to destroy their assigned target using any method they want. Return gunfire to be expected. Explosives recommended.

The final target, the last gasp of the Internet, will be the data centers, enormous windowless structures not designed for people, filled with servers that host the websites themselves. There are 6,190 data centers in total across 134 countries. United States alone has 2,269 of them.

With a little over 9,000 men, the third wave of Purists will be tasked with destroying their assigned data center in just thirty minutes, ideally finishing by 9:00 AM.

The four masterminds behind the operation, Jax, Munt, Bro and Lossy, knew the chances of them destroying all 6,190 data centers were astronomical. As a failsafe, they assigned 2,000 of those third wave Purists on eight specific targets, the so-called "super data centers." Together they hold the vast majority of the Internet. There's one in New York City, one in Los Angeles, one in Miami, one in Palo Alto, two in London and two in Paris. If they managed to destroy just those eight targets, the Internet would be crippled beyond comprehension.

The proper authorities will finally put a stop to the 11/11 Attacks around 8:55 AM GMT. The damage will be as follows: 12,524 Purists killed — including masterminds Munt Bloom and Lossy Berkowitz — in addition to 51,102 security guards and roughly 4,000 civilians. All 805 cables, 4,900 root server sites, and 900 data centers destroyed, including all eight super data centers.

In just 55 minutes, 80% of the Internet had been deleted, including the entirety of Wikipedia, YouTube, TrueSwitch and everything older than 2040.

The world will never get that data back.

President-Elect Cameron will be expected to condemn that a widespread act of violence and terrorism, but having spent the past year making himself synonymous with the Unplugged philosophy, he knows no one will believe a word of it. He was trapped in a lie of his own making.

Mad out of his wits, Cameron will attempt to end his association with the Unplugged Movement, blaming Esabell for putting him in that awful position.

Esabell, fighting to survive, will pull every excuse from the book. She'll claim Quentin was the original mastermind behind the 11/11 Attacks, the Manifesto being proof of his disturbed mind. She'll claim, upon learning what Quentin and Jax were planning, that she had ousted them from the Movement herself, determined to redirect its philosophy away from the Manifesto and instead toward Assimilation, i.e. peaceful digital and non-digital existence. Cameron won't believe a word of her ramblings, but Esabell will drop the panic and tell him to use that narrative to save his ass, promising it will work. Cameron won't like seeing Esabell's true colors like that, but since he had nothing better to suggest, he'll allow her one last chance to redeem herself.

On the afternoon of November 12, 2048, President-Elect Douglas Cameron will take the podium outside the ruins of Palo Alto's super data center and deliver a carefully curated speech, his rigid body ready to vomit from the phoniness alone, mourning the fallen security guards that gave their lives, condemning the cruel Radicals responsible for such a devastating attack, and taking the time to absolve Esabell's Unplugged Movement of any perceived blame. He'll pause for applause, making sure to flash Esabell, that two-faced cunt standing just behind him, a nasty resentful look. Because of her, he became the very thing he accused Quentin of being: a charlatan. Peddling a bogus philosophy. Pretending to believe his own manure.

At the other end of the plaza, on the fourth floor of an abandoned warehouse, Cal Vectors will aim the crosshairs of his rifle at Douglas Cameron's heart and pull the trigger.

Shots will ring out, the crowd screaming, running around like mad. Blood will blast out of Cameron's back as he groans, warm spray hitting Esabell's shocked face. A second shot will ring out, and with a hard CRUNCH, skull and brain matter will blow out the back of Cameron's head, his corpse falling to the ground.

The Secret Service will storm the warehouse in seconds, guns drawn. Cal will reload, pointing his rifle now at the only set of stairs, thrilled he actually got him, he actually got the son of a bitch. Best of all, he was right. Cameron *was* planning something in Vermont. They *were* all in on it. He was right! He was *right!*

Secret Service heads will poke up the stairs and Cal will shoot first, backing up against the wall. The agents will return fire, a bullet hitting Cal in the shoulder. A wave of pain will kill Cal's adrenaline, and he'll suddenly be overwhelmed with fear. He'll drop the gun and try to run, dashing toward the light like a coward, only to overshoot the balcony's edge, flip over the railing and fall four stories. His back will break on the concrete, and he'll die in pain. No thought. Just pain.

As Esabell watches Cameron's assassin fall four stories, a harsh realization will hit her, the same one Quentin had at his last Assimalist meeting: It's over.

Sure enough, Grover Mills — Cameron's running mate, now President-Elect — will immediately distance himself from Esabell Cortina-Gomez out of fear for his own life, thus ending the Unplugged Movement overnight.

The coroners will find a manifesto tucked inside Cal's shirt pocket, hand-scrawled ramblings that he killed Cameron out of retaliation for his assassination of Quentin Wagner and his secret role in planning the 11/11 Attacks. What's left of the Anti-Unplugged will immediately disband, desperate to distance themselves from that psycho lunatic, and they'll move on with their lives with no problems whatsoever.

Esabell Cortina-Gomez, too exhausted to pick up the pieces and start all over, will move back to California. She'll find herself a safe man with a good job and have two kids, settling a quiet, simple, *mellow* life.

A Congressional committee will investigate where that doctored Quentin Wagner suicide video came from, it being the chief inspiration behind Cal Vector's vendetta against Douglas Cameron according to his brother Jim. Its origins will be traced back to the DCC computer of one Jaymeigh Grady-Smith-Waterhouse-Price, which at the time of the video's creation was in the possession of her former assignment, Representative Natasha Mnozhynskyi. To make matters worse, investigators will also find a printed series of fake emails between Jaymeigh and Natasha inside Cal Vector's apartment, dated after Jaymeigh had already resigned from the DCC and yet sent from the very same laptop.

Despite overwhelming pressure from all sides, Natasha will stubbornly refuse to resign, forcing a formal vote of expulsion that will bring Ms. M's twenty-eight years in office to a shameful end.

After a lengthy investigation and a public trial, Jax Halsteder and Bro Williams, the two surviving masterminds of the 11/11 Attacks, will each receive life sentences at Guantanamo Bay. There, Jax will be the happiest he's ever been. All his meals prepared for him. No need for a real job or a closet full of skills. Just free room and board and all the respect he could ever ask for.

Every so often, a fellow inmate will ask Jax and Bro how they did it. How did they plan the largest terrorist attack in human history? How did they coordinate the individual movements of 20,000 people across 143 countries? How did they know the 8,492 targets they needed to kill the Internet?

But Jax won't give them a straight answer, and neither will Bro. Because they know what would happen if they spoke the truth, how dead they'll be once their acolytes, those proud life-long Purists still out there, found out their dirty little secret.

How did they pull it off? Simple.

They used the Internet.

15.

legacy

Without the Internet, seventeen years will go by like minutes. All the infrastructure the Purists destroyed on 11/11 will be rebuilt at great cost to what was used to be known as the Hateful Eight, only the world won't want to go back to the Internet anymore — the privileged First World, at least. By 2065, the Internet will be synonymous with cheap, the only countries still on it being the ones that can't afford high quality luxuries like newspapers, postage and in-person retail.

To keep up with the large demand of paper-based news and entertainment, entire rainforests will have to be bulldozed. A successor to SETA will pass allowing unsolicited advertising on the insides of books. People will bitch and moan about it at first, but without digital echo chambers to flock to, they'll learn to accept it faster, and the revenue will come pouring in.

In the first years after the Unplugged Movement's official end date, the world won't really know how to interpret the whole thing. An informal reactionary movement will start up, a nameless trend of stability, happiness, and gratitude. But over time, that era of peace will no longer be considered a reaction to what came before; instead, it'll be considered a direct result of it. And so, by the late 2050s, nostalgia for the Unplugged Movement will grow. Patch-covered denim will be in vogue once again. Ear gauging will return in a much more aesthetically pleasing way. "Unplugger" will become a generic Halloween costume, "Unplugged" a general party theme. Anyone still holding resentment for those violent Unpluggers, the ones that perpetrated 11/11, will be seen as out of touch, moronic, stuck in the past.

And as those Unplugged nostalgists get older, increased demand for firsthand stories will rise. Esabell Cortina-Gomez will suddenly receive calls out of the blue asking for her side of the story. Jax Halsteder will receive visits at his new facility, bags of letters offering millions for an exclusive tell-all. And after Jax and Esabell tell their stories ad nauseum, their perspectives unchanged after all those years, a fresh take, a new take, will soon be asked for.

Phibs Cantell, forty-two years old with intense LASIKed eyes and a permanent frown, will walk on the set of the new Unplugged-themed documentary from an ambitious first-time female director: established D.C. insider Jaymeigh Grady-Smith-Waterhouse-Price.

"Thank you for agreeing to speak with us, Amphibian," Jaymeigh will say, shaking his hand.

"Phibs."

"*Phibs.* I'm sorry."

"It's alright." Phibs will sit in his assigned chair under the harsh lights, Jaymeigh's makeup artist coming over to put on the final touches.

Jaymeigh will sit across from Phibs, smoothing out her suit. "With *First Gauge*, I want to focus on Unplugged's early days, before the Boycott, to provide context for everything that came after."

Phibs will look at her with uneasily. "You're not gonna talk about the Festival?"

"Too much has been done on that already. Well... as much as can be done, considering there's no firsthand footage of it."

"I see." Phibs will shoo the makeup artist away.

"I'm more interested in the truth anyway. There's quite a lot of misconceptions about Unplugged."

"Like what?"

Jaymeigh will shrug. "The First Gauge for example. In the later years there was a bit of confusion as to who actually hole-punched their ear on November 25th—"

"Esabell."

Jaymeigh will stare. "No?"

"Yes." Phibs will adjust his ass on that shitty chair.

Jaymeigh will furrow her brow. "I know it wasn't Esabell."

"Well, I'm saying it was. I was there. I would know."

Jaymeigh won't have any clue how to respond to that.

Phibs will shrug. "Esabell was the Unplugged Movement. She wrote the Manifesto, humbly refusing to take credit for it. She started the Coalition. She put Quentin on *The Evening Show*. She founded the Happy Child Campaign and raised millions of dollars to put an end to cyberbullying despite Quentin's many attempts to stop her. She founded the News-letter, first of its kind, single-handedly reviving the newspaper industry. She made the Unplugged Festival happen, again de-spite Quentin repeatedly trying to stop it. And she saved the Movement by ousting Quentin and Jax when she found out they were planning 11/11."

Jaymeigh's lips will clench a bit. She'll pull pieces of paper from her bag and hold them out for Phibs to take. "Then why, on the day of the Festival, did you co-author an editorial in Quentin's email newsletter condemning the Loyalists for falsely crediting Esabell for the First Gauge?"

Phibs will stare at Jaymeigh mysteriously, refusing to even look at the papers in her hand. "Where did you find those?" he'll ask slowly.

"Answer the question."

"Where did you find those?"

Jaymeigh will hesitate. "An ex-Assimalist extracted them from his personal hard drive. They cost me a fortune, believe me." She'll will hold the emails out further. "Please, answer the question."

Phibs will take a deep breath. "Turn off the camera."

"It's off."

"Turn off the camera."

Jaymeigh will look at the camera next to her, aimed right at Phibs. "It's literally off."

"Point it away then."

Jaymeigh will softly nudge the camera 90° to the right.

"Thank you." Phibs will fold his hands. "I did some digging on you as well."

"Answering the fucking question, Amphibian."

"You were Ms. M's Chaperone, were you not?"

Jaymeigh will say nothing.

Phibs will nod. "Tell me, what's your agenda with this?"

"I don't have an agenda."

"Everyone has an agenda."

"I want to know what really happened."

"No one cares what really happened. What's your agenda with this film?"

Jaymeigh will hesitate. "I want to know why she did it, alright? I want to know what happened to her to make her think she had no other choice than to deepfake a suicide video and get a Republican elected President. I want to know how she got to the point of thinking that was normal. But I don't want to fit some pre-fixed conclusion, I want to know what really happened. For once, the truth actually is my agenda. So stop bullshitting me. Esabell Cortina-Gomez was not the secret mastermind behind Unplugged. The Unplugged Festival, the Happy Child Campaign, the 11/11 Attacks, Douglas Cameron's assassination, none of that was what Quentin Wagner stood for, was it? His philosophy had been warped by outside forces, the same forces that warped Natasha's. I just want to know what they were. I want to know how a simple TrueSwitch post asking the world to stop using the Internet got bastardized into a generational pissing contest that got 68,000 people killed and a President assassinated."

Phibs will stare for a bit. "President-*Elect*."

"Yes, President-Elect. You know what I mean."

"Why didn't you say it, though? Was it because you knew your point wouldn't have hit as hard had you left that out?"

Jaymeigh will hesitate.

"That's how it starts," Phibs will murmur. "Imagine *that* getting out of your control." He'll pull out a pack of cigarettes. "So let's talk about what we *can* control." He'll light one up. Blow out smoke. "We peaked early, you and I. All of us did. Anything we do for the rest of our lives won't change the fact that 'Unplugged' will be somewhere in the headline of our obituaries. What we did in our twenties will be the only thing anyone wants to remember us for. Right now we're being celebrated for it. But one day, we won't. One day, an entire generation will hate us for taking the Internet away from them. And if we play our cards wrong, we'll live to see that happen. Do you really want to be most remembered for your complacency in Natasha's Bill? Your complacency in her making that video, the one that got a President — I'm sorry, *President-Elect* — killed?" Phibs will pause. "Do I want to be remembered for turning on the only member of the Coalition that actually succeeded in what they wanted to do, siding instead with a dying remnant of a decent thing? No, I don't. That might be what happened. That might be the truth. But that wouldn't do us any good, would it?"

Jaymeigh will withdraw within herself. "There's a time for judgment and a time for objectivity. It's still too soon to judge any of us."

"That doesn't stop people, does it?"

"I don't care. They're wrong. Quentin Wagner was the only one morally right about everything. People need to know the real Esabell."

"The real Esabell made Unplugged a success."

"The real Esabell did not commit the First Gauge. She did not co-write the Manifesto. I know how tempting it is for us to put on rose-colored glasses to keep control of the narrative, but that is exactly what Natasha Mnozhynskyi did and look what happened. To her, the truth was nothing but an inconvenience." Jaymeigh will pause. "I don't want to be like that."

Phibs will lean back in his chair. "But you did want to be her at one point."

"I wanted to be Ms. M. She wasn't real."

"Ms. M was the perfect Natasha. The strong Natasha. The one that inspired you to work harder, to study harder, to learn an entirely new field. If you had known the real Natasha, you never would've done that. The real Natasha was weak. The moment she lost control of the narrative, she did everything she could to try and get it back. I'm in the same boat as you. The Quentin I loved, the Quentin that inspired me, who gave me life and strength, who pulled me out of obscurity and anx-iety, he wasn't real either. You wanna know who the real Quentin was? The real Quentin was a fucking loser. A basket case. A *liar*. He wasn't wise or smart. He was an emotional, antisocial nutjob, just like I was. And he had no plan, *no plan*, to actually implement those changes he wanted for the world. What good would it have done if we only saw the real them? We needed them to be perfect so we could fix ourselves, to better ourselves. There's no good in us painting Unplugged exactly the way it was. We were a bunch of emotional kids way in over their head, hurting people and ruining lives. No one wants us to be that. They need us to be perfect. They need to know Unplugged was worth it, that everything good that hap-pened was exactly what we intended to happen. If history doesn't look like a perpetual improvement, then… honestly, what's the point of anything? Why get up in the morning if there used to be greatness and now there isn't? Why even try?"

Jaymeigh will stay silent, her will broken down.

"Like you said," Phibs will say, flicking ash on the ground. "There's a time for judgment and a time for objectivity. The world's not ready for us to be objective. Until then, they need someone else to tell them how to judge it." He'll shrug. "So what will the history books read?"

Six months later, *First Gauge* will premiere to rave re-views. Critics will call it an essential time capsule, *the* cultural cornerstone, of what is only referred to now as the Unplugged Generation.

Jaymeigh Grady-Smith-Waterhouse-Price will win the Academy Award for Best Documentary Feature, and she'll in-vite Esabell Cortina-Gomez to join her on stage, and Esabell will smile and wave humbly as the crowd gives her a standing ovation, and Jaymeigh will use her speech to laude Esabell's great contributions to society. And in the months that follow, Esabell will suddenly find herself winning lifetime achievement after lifetime achievement. And her kids will be so proud of her. They'll say, "Our mom is Esabell Cortina-Gomez. She's a fucking hero."

But in the dark smoked-filled rooms of college campuses, different stories will be told. Stories of a world connected as one. A world of magic. Of mystery. An entire library in the palm of your hand. Music playing without a disc or a wire. Entire movies, a wealth of information, right there in your pocket. Small towns in virtual space where everyone can share their thoughts without censorship. A world without postage, ads, or pricey paper. A green world. A digital world. What they used to call the Internet. If only it was still around, just the way it was in its prime. How great would that be?

Quentin would've been forty-five.

Ø.

coda

But not today. Today he's four, sleeping in his bed, his whole life ahead of him.

And I'm lying here, my husband sleeping next to me. Too exhausted to think anymore. Too stressed out to sleep. What if I'm wrong? What if my decision to raise Quentin exclusively in the analog world, the way I was raised, ended up being the very thing that ruined his life? That ruined the world? Is it really so wrong to let him go online every now and then? Is there really anything wrong with him being just like everyone else?

Every decision I make for him will change him. Everything I let him see will change him. Everything I explain to him will be all he knows. How can I prepare him for a future I don't even know myself? What if it's nothing like I imagine it to be? What if it's worse? What if it's better?

I can't do this. I can't make these decisions for him. But I have to. That's what being a father is. That's the job. And I have to be a good father. I just have to be. But I don't know what that means. I never had one. Or at least I don't think I did. Maybe I just… Oh God, I really can't do this.

Now I understand why everyone feels the need to bitch to school boards about what they're telling their kids to read, why they feel the need to make such a big stink about what they're teaching them. But all that is is wasted effort. None of it will change anything. It won't matter. It might even make things worse. He's gonna see what he sees anyway, right? So I should just let him. Right? Isn't that better than forcing a lens on him against his will? Maybe I *don't* know everything. Maybe I *am* wrong about things.

But isn't that doing nothing? I can't do nothing, right? I have to have some sort of standard. I can't be neglectful. Because that's wrong too, right? Is this neglect?

How am I supposed to do this?

How does *anybody* do this?

from the publisher

Thank you so much for reading *unplugged*. This one was a lot of fun to write, something very different from my norm. I'm very happy it came out exactly as I intended.

I believe the most interesting stories are those with personality, intelligence, and just a bit of strange. That can only be possible with a singular creative voice. I chose to self-publish my novels through David Schulze Books so I could tell my stories without compromising my final cut privileges.

All I ask in return is an **honest** review on Amazon, Goodreads, B&N.com, or the social media platform of your choice. Doing so not only provides feedback I can use on future projects, it also directly supports my growth as a career author.

If you want to mention this book on Facebook, Twitter, or Instagram, don't forget to add #unplugged or #DavidSchulze. Thanks again, and I hope you read more of my work.

— david schulze

about the author

David Schulze (né Stehman) was born and raised in Phoenixville, Pennsylvania. A lifelong admirer of movies, mythology, and classic literature, David loves stories across all mediums.

In 2017, David graduated from Emerson College with a BA in Writing for Film and Television and a Minor in Literature. He has written nine feature screenplays and four shorts, many of them placing in screenwriting competitions. Falling back on his love of prose, David adapted his ninth feature, *The Sins of Jack Branson* (2018 Final Draft Big Break Contest Quarterfinalist) as his debut novel in 2021. His critically acclaimed second novel *Andrezj of Hollywood* was the 2024 IPPY Bronze Medalist for West Pacific Fiction, and his novella *unplugged* was selected as one of *Kirkus Reviews'* 100 Best Indie Books of 2024.

David lives in Marlton, New Jersey and Sarasota, Florida with his husband Howie.

For exclusive stories, in-depth analyses, and updates on future projects, go to davidschulzebooks.com